SAUSAGEY SANTA

I0629324

CARLTON MELLICK III

ERASERHEAD PRESS
PORTLAND, OREGON

ERASERHEAD PRESS
205 NE BRYANT
PORTLAND, OR 97211

WWW.ERASERHEADPRESS.COM

ISBN: 1-62105-077-7

Printed in the USA.

AUTHOR'S NOTE

Like most American families, I was raised as a non-churchgoing Christian. This means that we were not religious at all, but celebrated all Christian holidays. We didn't talk about Jesus. Ever. Christmas was all about Santa Claus. We were Santaists. So, growing up as a kid, Santa seemed far more real than Jesus ever was. Same goes for the Easter Bunny and Tooth Fairy. These three mythological figures actually visited my house. They interacted with me on a personal level. They were totally real to me. And our parents are awesome for lying to us about them. Though one thing that always boggles my mind is how a kid can still believe in God after they learn that Santa isn't real. Santa was a much bigger loss to me as a kid.

"So Santa isn't real?" I asked my mom.

"Sorry, he's not real. Don't tell your sister," she said.

"What about the Easter Bunny and Tooth Fairy?"

"They're not real either. None of them are real."

"So God's fake, too, huh?"

"No, God's real."

"What? Are you serious? God seems the most make-believe of all of them!"

"Yeah, God and Satan exist. It's just the fun ones that are fake."

Sometimes I wonder if God and Satan and Heaven and Hell weren't all made up by parents thousands of years ago in order to make their children behave. It seems exactly like a parental stunt. They tell the kids that if they're good they'll get to go to a magical happy place after they die, but if they're bad they'll have to go to a horrible place filled with fire and scary monsters. Back then, parents would bring their kids to temples and giggle in the back of the room as the preachers scared the hell out of their kids. Then whenever the kids acted up the parents would just have to bring up what the preacher said and the kids would immediately fall back in line.

Personally, I think this would be hilarious if it were actually how it all started. But it might be even funnier if it were on the cosmic scale, where all living humans are viewed as children until they die and enter the afterlife.

After death, you meet some guy in a white suit.

You say, "Are you God? Is this Heaven?"

He says, "Have a seat. There's something I need to tell you."

You sit down.

He says, "I'm sorry, but God really doesn't exist."

"What about Satan?"

"He doesn't either. None of it exists. I'm sorry."

He sees the disappointed look on your face and gives you a hug.

"Don't tell your sister. She's still alive and we wouldn't want to ruin it for her."

So seven years ago I wrote the novel Sausagey Santa for the Santaist audience. Even though I've written about thirty books since then, it still remains one of my favorite novellas. I think it's the main character that still speaks to me. The Sly Guy is one smooth dude. He is loosely based after my dad, who used to always moonwalk from room to room, making guns with his fingers, and singing along to *Mack the Knife* while dancing with himself. We thought he was a total dork but we loved him for it.

Here it is. The reissue of Sausagey Santa. I hope you enjoy it.

—Carlton Mellick III 10/4/2013 11:07pm

CHAPTER ONE
TELEVISION CAKE

I never should have married a woman named Decapitron.

It's more like the name of an evil transformer than the name of a wife. Her given name was Susanne Lewis, but she has gone by Decapitron ever since she was a little kid and got it legally changed when she turned eighteen. I'd prefer if she went by Susanne but she says she'll annihilate me if I ever call her by that name.

I should have listened to my mom when she told me "you just can't trust a woman named Decapitron." She was right. Decapitron is unpredictable. She's like a flesh-bag of nitroglycerin that's ready to explode at the drop of a hat.

I could have married any woman. When I was younger, the ladies were always swooning over me. I could have had any of them. I could have married a supermodel. Maybe I never should have married any woman at all and stayed a swinging bachelor for the rest of my life. I mean, I'm a wild man. I have one of the most stylish hairdos anyone has ever seen. I call my hairstyle 'the sly guy' and I like to make guns with my fingers and point them at people when I walk down the sidewalk.

It's Christmas Eve. I'm in the living room bobbing my head to *Jingle Bell Rock* while drinking brandy eggnog out of a snowman-shaped mug, trying to figure out a way to work off my beer belly without actually doing any exercise. Decapitron is in the kitchen with the twins baking a cake for Jesus's birthday tomorrow. It's one of her stupid family's stupid traditions. On Christmas Day, she always lights candles on a cake and forces us to sing Happy Birthday to Jesus. She puts up balloons and party decorations, with a banner that reads HAPPY BIRTHDAY, JESUS! stretched across the dining room wall.

It's pretty awesome that her family was killed in a car accident early this year. I can finally enjoy my Christmas without having to listen to her dwarfish father's racist jokes or her mother's retarded opinions concerning the sexiness of women with hairy armpits (namely, herself). They should have had the decency to die years ago, like my parents did. My parents rocked. They knew how to get morbidly obese in their youth and die middle-aged. I hope to be just like them.

I chug down the nog and sneak over to the Christmas tree to check out my presents. The Christmas tree is about seventeen feet high and ten feet wide. We get a bigger tree every year. Decapitron cut a hole in the ceiling just so we could fit bigger trees into our house at Christmas time. Upstairs, in our bedroom, the top of the tree comes out of the floor and forms another full-sized tree near the foot of our bed. She says she likes the smell of pine trees when she wakes up in the morning.

I squat down and crawl underneath the enormous tree, pretending like I am exploring a vast cavern full of colorfully-patterned rocks. Examining the rocks... Hmm, there doesn't seem to be many presents for me under here. Decapitron usually only gets me one thing for Christmas: piercings. She's got a metal fetish and ever since we started dating she's forced me to get more and more things pierced. Not my face, mind you. She doesn't think a good family man should have piercings that show, so all fifty-six of my piercings are concealed under my clothing. My entire torso is completely studded. It's like I'm covered in steel freckles.

I don't want any piercings. I don't really like them. Decapitron forces me to get them, though. She tells me that if I ever even think about removing any of my piercings she will annihilate me.

There's really only two things I want for Christmas: 1) Cannibal Death Cop on DVD and 2) the new Spelunker CD.

Spelunker is my favorite band ever. They are the leading group of a new genre of music called Adventure Rock. It is the kind of music that Indiana Jones would listen to if he was a real person. Adventure Rock bands sing about cool stuff like archeology, mountain climbing, wilderness survival, cave exploration, anthropological studies, kayaking, and swimming around in sunken pirate ships while fighting off man-eating sharks and terrorists with spear guns. Nothing gets me more pumped than listing to Spelunker while driving my sports utility vehicle to work every day.

But I doubt I'm getting the CD for Christmas. I never get what I want. I'll probably have to buy it for myself next month.

Decapitron wants the same thing for Christmas every year: transformer toys.

She actually really does think of herself as an evil transformer. She even has a secret Decepticon tattoo on her shoulder that you have to rub in order to see it. Ever since she was a kid she wanted to be an evil robot that could transform into different things. At first she wanted to be able to transform into a space ship. Then she wanted to be able to transform into an electric boa constrictor. Then a laser cannon. Then a monster truck. Then a guillotine, so she could actually decapitate people.

These days she wishes she could transform into a nuclear submarine. She could do a lot of damage if she could turn into a nuclear submarine.

"What are you doing under there?" an angry voice says to me.

I look back to see a small tapping foot outside of the Christmas tree.

"You're not allowed in there."

It's my daughter, Nora.

"Coming," I say, needles poking into my hands and elbows as I crawl out from under the tree, knocking ornaments down as my back brushes against the lower branches.

I peek out from under the tree like a bad dog hiding under a bed. She stares down at me with a disgusted look on her face. Blue and green lights sparkle against her braces.

"How many times do I have to warn you?" she says, wiping the open wound on the side of her face with a towel. "You go under there one more time and I'm going to have Mom return all of your presents."

Even though she's seven years old, Nora is the boss of the family. I'm pretty sure she is the anti-Christ, which is why I don't fuck with her. Even Decapitron doesn't dare defy the kid. It's probably the gory black growth on the side of her head that makes her seem so damned scary. It's a morbid balloon of flesh shaped like an adult male hand growing out of her brain and gripping the side of her skull. It is constantly pulsating and bleeding, and requires constant care. The doctor said she probably wouldn't live to see her first birthday, but that son of a bitch didn't know what he was talking about. I should have sued his ass. If I knew she was going to live this long I probably would have given her up for adoption years ago.

For Christmas, Nora asked for a neural implant so she could plug her brain directly into the computer. Technology is advancing so quickly these days that it's hard to keep up with all the inventions. First, there was the Internet. Then came holographic movies. Then helicopter backpacks. Then laser eyes. Now they invented a way to plug computers directly into your brain. You can upload 110 MB of knowledge an hour into your mind now or you can download your memories onto a disc so that you'll never forget them.

It's all still pretty new. Not a lot of people can afford the surgery yet and there's a lot of skepticism about its safety. A few people at work have done it because the company paid for the operation. They say that in about five years everyone will have it done and no company will hire you without it. I really hope they are wrong. My employer already owns most of my time, all I need is for them to own part of my brain too.

Unfortunately, we couldn't afford to get Nora the operation for Christmas. It's so far out of our budget it's ridiculous. We'd have to put a second mortgage on our house. I don't even know if it is legal for minors to get the implant. She's going to be fucking pissed tomorrow morning and I know she's going to blame me. My punishment will probably be pretty severe this time. If I'm lucky she won't let me have any of my piercings for Christmas. Or maybe she'll make me go to my room during Jesus's birthday party.

Nora sits down on a chair in front of the tree, guarding the presents.

"Suck in your gut," she tells me.

I do as she commands but let it slack when I turn away from her, calling her a fucking witch under my breath. "Rudolf The Red-Nosed Reindeer" is now playing on the stereo. It is a funky disco mix version. I pour myself some more eggnog and groove across the horsehair carpet into the kitchen.

Decapitron is putting the finishing touches on Jesus's birthday cake. The twins are strapped to her back gurgling at each other. Both boys were born with full heads of hair that now look like large globs of cotton candy. My wife decided to dye each of their heads a different fruity color. Matt Jr. has neon green hair. Decapitron Jr. has turquoise blue hair. Matt Jr. goes by Greeny or Matty. Decapitron Jr. goes by Bluey or Tron or Voltron. We are considering changing his name to Voltron. Matty will probably go by Matt when he's older. My wife never calls me Matt anyway so there wouldn't be much confusion.

When I was younger I went by Sly Guy Matthew Fry, or Sly Fry for short. That's what I like to be called. But Decapitron and my kids just address me by my surname, Fry. My wife didn't take my last name when we got married, she doesn't have a last name at all, so it's not that strange when she calls me Fry. But it's weird when the kids do it. They don't call me Dad or Matthew or Sly Guy. I'm just Fry to them.

The twins are about two years old but they still look like they are infants. I'm not sure if they are ever going to grow up. Decapitron still breastfeeds them. She has them holstered on her back so she can whip them out like shotguns or samurai swords whenever it's time for them to feed. She wears a breakaway top designed for strippers so that she can rip it open and fling them towards her breasts in the blink of an eye.

I think she has been breastfeeding them for so long because it turns her on. I'm not positive about this, but she's a weird fucking woman so I wouldn't put it past her. She has pierced nipples and likes to have them sucked, especially while she's lactating. I know because she usually forces me to drink from her nipples while we have sex. I'm pretty sure the doctor told her she shouldn't keep her piercings in, but there's no arguing with Decapitron. I used to tell her that the kids would turn out funny if she breastfeeds them for too long, but she just tells me to shut up or she will annihilate me.

Decapitron is always threatening to annihilate me. And she could do it, too. Easily. She annihilates people for a living. By day, her job is housewife. But by night, she earns a living as a death sport street fighter.

She only fights about two or three times a year and usually makes a few hundred grand a match. It is all illegal, of course. Her sponsors are a French mafia family that sends her all over the world to fight in private tournaments. Most of the matches are not officially bouts to the death, but whenever my wife fights the match is always to the death. She never allows any of her opponents to survive, because her finishing maneuver is a powerful roundhouse kick that causes decapitation. After all, she has to live up to her name. The audience always loves her. They are there to see fatalities and she never fails to give them some.

Our relationship was pretty much built on fear. It started out as just a crazy sexual escapade. Me with my irresistible hairdo and super slick dance moves. Decapitron with her black makeup and tight leather outfits. She was instantly attracted to me, as most of the ladies were, and aggressively came on to me at a nightclub. I never slept with a dominatrix type before, so I decided to give her a try. One night of wild sex, that's all I wanted out of her. But I made the mistake of bringing her back to my place. Once she knew where I lived, she kept coming back for more. Next thing I knew she was calling me her boyfriend and I didn't know how to get her out of my life.

The day she presumed I was about to try to break up with her she decided to show me what she did for a living. I had no idea what her job was. She didn't look like a fighter. She never had any scars. She was very tall and in great shape, but she wasn't all that muscular. The next thing I knew she was beating the utter piss out of a 400 pound tank of a Russian. This guy was a behemoth of muscle and platinum chest hair. Bigger than any wrestler or football player I've ever seen. Bigger than any boxer. If I saw him in the wild I'd think he was the abominable snowman.

But Decapitron made short work of him. Without ever getting touched, she broke his ribs, cracked open his ankle, crushed his liver, shattered his foot, ripped a tendon out of his arm, and then decapitated him with her toes.

After they dragged the corpse away, she told me, "If you ever leave me I will annihilate you."

So instead of breaking up with her we got married and started making kids.

I lean against the counter and check out the cake. *How The Grinch Stole Christmas* is playing on the surface. Right now it's on the part where the Grinch encounters Mary Loo Who and is trying to come up with an excuse for stealing her family's Christmas tree.

The cake is a television cake. It is one of the most popular styles in this new era of hi-tech cake design. The icing of a television cake has the ability to pick up images from satellite TV and display them on your cake. You just have to tell the satellite company which channel you want on your cake and they charge your credit card by the hour until you cancel the service. You can't control the volume on the icing but it's usually not too loud or too quiet. The show continues playing while you eat the cake, but you won't be able to see the whole screen anymore. I don't like to eat television cake. I just watch it while the family cuts pieces away. It kind of freaks me out.

The weird part of it is that the show still plays inside of you after you've eaten it. Whenever Decapitron eats her cake she always opens her mouth to show me the chewed up TV show. Sometimes she puts her belly to my ear so I can hear the muffled sounds of the show's characters inside of her. But worst of all, she likes to freak me out by leaving floaters in the toilet after she's eaten the cake. She knows that poop covered in sparkling television static bothers the heck out of me.

The technical advancement in cakes is sure impressive, but I prefer to eat good old fashioned German chocolate cake. You just can't improve on that.

CHAPTER TWO
CHAINSAW ANGEL WINGS

I don't hate every member of my family. Well, I wouldn't hate any of them if they weren't so difficult to like. But there is one of them that I love. My second daughter, Angelica. My little angel. Decapitron likes to think of Angelica and Matty as my kids, and Nora and Voltron as her kids. If we separated and I was allowed to live that's probably how the family would be split up.

Angelica is upstairs coloring pictures of Santa's workshop, wearing angel wings made out of chainsaw blades. My wife made them for her. She thinks they are pretty cool. Being only five, Angelica doesn't know exactly what chainsaws are for. She just thinks of them as very heavy metal angel wings. Just like Decapitron she is surprisingly strong and has no problem wearing chainsaw blades around the house.

"Hi, Sly Fry," Angelica says as I moonwalk into her room. She's the only one who sometimes calls me Sly Fry.

I point gun-fingers at her and wink.

"Wanna see what I colored?" she asks.

"Sure, honey bunny."

She shows me a picture of elves wrapping presents. The whole page is purple. She only colors with purple crayons because that's her favorite color.

"Awesome," I tell her.

She shows me five more pages of her coloring book, all of them purple. Her purple crayon is just a tiny nub. Soon she's going to have to color with the red and blue crayon squeezed together.

"It's almost story time," I tell her.

"Santa stories?"

"Yeah, Santa stories."

I hold her hand as we go down the stairs. Decapitron and the other kids are waiting for us impatiently. Nora taps her wrist at me, as if she's ever worn a watch in her life.

Besides singing Happy Birthday to Jesus, Decapitron has a few other stupid Christmas traditions she forces on us. One of them is to have crab balls filled with mushrooms and vodka sauce for dinner on Christmas Eve. I liked the crab balls okay when her mother used to make them, but Decapitron puts a spin on the recipe that completely ruins them. Instead of putting a dab of vodka in the creamy tomato sauce she puts a glass of vodka, two shots of rum, a shot of gin, a shot of tequila, and ¾ cup cognac. It is the Long Island Iced Tea of sauces. But unlike Long Islands, her sauce tastes like shit. The only reason to eat her crab balls is to get wasted. Unfortunately, the alcohol and the shellfish never sit right together in my stomach. I've been holding back a puke all night.

Another tradition she has is to make dozens and dozens of snowmen in the yard. Every year, we wake up early the day before Christmas and construct an army of them. But they aren't the jolly nice kind of snowmen. They are freaky weird snowmen. Some of them have nails for hair, others have axe limbs and steel wool beards. Some have shoes for breasts. Some have fan blades for faces. Some have pineapple horns, sledgehammer heads, or telephone chord tentacles. It takes most of the day to make them and they fill the yard like some kind of grotesque crowd of frozen mutants. The kids have fun but I dread constructing them every year. I'm the one who rolls the balls of snow. They are the ones who get to decorate the faces with items from the house. Decapitron always says it just wouldn't feel like Christmas without them.

My wife's favorite tradition is to sit around and tell Santa stories on Christmas Eve just before bed. It seems like a fun tradition when you think about it. I'm sure a lot of kids would like to hear tales of Rudolf, Frosty, Mr. and Mrs. Claus, presents, Santa's toy shop, elves, and winter wonderlands. But the problem is Decapitron doesn't tell any of those stories. Her family raised her to believe in a different Santa mythos. One that I find a bit disturbing and not suitable for kids.

Decapitron tells the story of Sausagey Santa.

She says it is the true story of Santa Claus. According to her, Santa was once a king of a small country who hated children and Jesus so much that he tried to outlaw both of them in his land. King Kringle was a ruthless tyrant who sent his armies from village to village burning down their churches. All children under the age of twelve were rounded up and shipped overseas to be sold into slavery. And all men were forbidden to impregnate their wives under the penalty of death.

This went on for only eighteen months until the citizenry picked up arms and conquered Kringle's armies. But he was not killed. His people instead left his punishment up to God.

The Almighty Lord decided to damn Kris Kringle to an immortal life. He would spend eternity spreading holy joy and cheer to the children of the world by delivering them presents every Christmas Eve. It was a living hell for the ex-king. He attempted suicide several times, but he just couldn't die. Whenever he chopped off his head or got his reindeer to quarter him, the elves would just sew him back together and send him on his way. The elves were master craftsmen and there was no organ in Santa's body that they couldn't fix no matter how damaged it became.

For his final suicide attempt, he put his body through a meat grinder. This mulched him up into a thick paste that he was sure could never be put back together again. For a couple days, he thought he'd succeeded. The elves didn't know how to reassemble him. But then after much discussion, the elves just remade him into a new shape. They stuffed his meat goo into sausage casings and linked them all together until they formed a man.

Kringle never attempted suicide again after that. It was bad enough he had to live an eternity as a collection of sausage balloons. He didn't want to make it any worse. After a few hundred years, Kringle started to enjoy his work. Kids didn't bother him anymore. Jesus stopped being a big part of Christmas. His personality changed from a sour wicked tyrant into a happy jolly soul. When he laughs, his body parts jiggle like balloons filled with meat jelly.

Then he changed his name to Sausagey Santa, or just Santa for short.

Decapitron tells the tale to the children, widening her green and yellow cat eyes as she speaks. She tells it more like a ghost story than a happy children's fantasy. But the kids never get scared. They get excited. They don't care that she describes Santa as a horrible tyrant turned jolly meat creature. They just care that he brings them presents.

"But Momma, how does Santa get down the chimney?" Angelica asks.

"He greases himself up with orange marmalade," Decapitron says. "And he's inflammable so the fire never burns him."

"But Momma," Angelica says, stretching her arms around her chainsaw wings, "how does he get around to every house in the world all in one night?"

"He rides in a sleigh made out of lightning," Nora injects with an uppity tone, as if her little sister is a complete retard for not already possessing the knowledge. "He can travel at the speed of light."

Angelica nods her head in agreement, pretending she knows all about the speed of light.

The twins are passed out on the couch and Nora's eyes are getting weak and droopy, probably from all the blood she lost while running around in the snow today. Decapitron decides it's time for everyone go to bed, but Angelica is wide awake and wants to hear more stories.

"Santa won't come if you don't go to sleep," Decapitron says. "He's hideously deformed and doesn't like kids to see him in his sausagey state."

"Ahhh, but Momma..." Angelica cries.

"Help Momma put out oysters and chips for Santa."

"What's that?" she asks.

"Sausagey Santa doesn't eat milk and cookies like mainstream culture thinks he does," Nora says, holding in her goopy head. "He likes deep fried oysters with freedom fries."

Nora calls them freedom fries because she's a big George W. Bush supporter.

"We also leave him a tall glass of coconut stout," I say, pouring a creamy beer into a large holiday stein.

"He doesn't drink on the job," Nora tells me.

"Well, just in case..." I say.

Decapitron flash fries some oysters and chips for a couple minutes, then puts them on a mistletoe-patterned paper plate and hands it to Angelica. My little chainsaw angel carries it out to the living room and sets it on the coffee table next to my frothy beer.

"It's just going to get flat," Nora says.

"Well, I bet you five candy canes that the stein will be empty by tomorrow morning."

Nora just puffs her lips at me. "I don't need to bet you. I know I'm right."

After Decapitron takes the kids up to bed, I chug Santa's beer until only foam remains. That'll teach the little freak not to question the sly man.

"Sly Fry: one, Nora: zero," I tell the fireplace.

I spin around on one foot and groove my way up the staircase, singing the hit Spelunker song "Sky Diving Escape Plan" in my head.

I'm lying in bed, waiting for Decapitron to get out of the bathroom.

Christmas time isn't so bad. It could be worse. I could be at work. My day job was supposed to be a dream of a career. I work as a video game designer for Nintendo. But it's really a piece of crap job that hardly pays and usually forces me to work long grueling hours in order to meet deadlines. I'm usually always working on the worst games, too. Most of them tend to get cancelled before their release. Right now I'm working on Video Foosball. Not only is it a retarded concept to make foosball into a high definition 3D holo-game, but the gameplay and controls are just horrid. You have to use both joysticks on the controller with each of your thumbs, and you control your goalie using your index fingers.

The only part of the game that I like is the facial expressions on the faces of the little bowling pin-shaped people that hit the ball. That was my idea. If they miss the ball their faces get sad or angry. If they hit the ball they get all excited and howl.

I have a feeling that after this game flops my career will be over.

There's one more Christmas Eve tradition that Decapitron forces me through every year. That is: Christmas sex. Every year she has to have some kind of Christmas-themed kinky sex.

Decapitron comes out of the bathroom wearing green and white holiday latex. Her hair is all tucked inside of a green rubber helmet strapped to her head. Deer antlers are attached to the sides of the helmet. They are real deer antlers, two feet high and nearly scraping the ceiling. Around her neck are reindeer bells. She's wearing dark green lipstick and eye makeup. She's even colored her eyebrows green.

"You didn't open your present," she says.

I look at the present near my feet.

"I was waiting for you," I say.

I open it up to find a matching green latex outfit. Only it is designed for a man and comes with a cape. Every year she buys us costumes for our Christmas Eve sex. They usually create a theme that we can roleplay. In the beginning, she didn't have me dress up as anything. She would usually just dress as a sexy Mrs. Claus for me. Then she had me dress up as a sexy Santa to go with her sexy Mrs. Claus. Then she had me dress as Mrs. Claus and dressed herself as Santa. Then she had us dress like Santa's elves. Then she dressed us up like snowmen. Then she had me dress like the nutcracker and she dressed as a music box ballerina and we did it inside a giant present. Last year she had us dress like Christmas candy and we did it inside of a giant stocking that was suspended from the ceiling.

This year we are reindeer. I put on my outfit for her, trying not to ruin my hairdo too much, and discover that my antlers aren't as big as hers. She probably likes the idea of having bigger antlers than me.

Decapitron puts on her vulture smile when she sees me in the outfit. Whenever we're about to have sex she has a weird smile on her face that I call her vulture smile.

"It's mating season in the winter forest," Decapitron says on all fours, looking at me from across the room.

She swipes her hand against the carpet like the front leg of a bull as it prepares to skewer a rodeo clown. Then she jumps to

27

her feet and charges at me with full speed, pointing her antlers at me.

"Holy fuck!" I scream as I see her barreling towards me.

I lower my head and her antlers crash into mine, throwing me back into the Christmas tree. My body thrashes the tree around and I can hear ornaments falling from the tree branches in the living room below.

"You have to do better than that," she tells me. "The winner of this contest gets the mate of his choosing."

I get to my feet and charge at her, hoping to stab her a little in the chest. She never takes it easy on me when we have sex and makes me pay for it if I ever take it easy on her. She sees me coming at her and starts charging towards me at full force.

Our antlers smash into each other. A loud clack vibrates through the room. She kicks me in the stomach and backs away. My belly explodes with pain and I fall to my knees. I look up at her. Blood is trickling out of her mouth. I must have nicked her lip when we clashed.

Decapitron charges at me again before I'm ready, but I get to my feet in time. We lock antlers. I push on her with all my strength and she pushes back, my heels sliding across the carpeting. She whips her head to the side, twisting my neck around, and forces me to the ground.

"Looks like I'm the alpha male," she says.

This is the time I know I need to fight back with all my strength or else she's going to get out her strap-on and fuck me in the ass to really show me that she's the man. I jerk my antlers around until they unlock from hers and then I plant them directly in her ribs. She yelps at me and kicks me in the face. I squirm away from her and she charges at me again. She backs me against a wall and then rams her antlers at my neck. They miss my neck, just barely. The antlers break through the wall next to each of my cheeks, trapping me between them.

Decapitron's breath is heavy against my chest. My breath is heavy against her forehead. I have heavy breaths because I am tired, she has heavy breaths because she is turned on. She pulls my penis out of a flap in the green latex and massages it. I can't see it but I know she has a vulture smile on her face.

We move to the bed and make love. She straps my wrists to the bedposts and pokes at my chest with her antlers as she fucks. Once she approaches orgasm the pokes turn into stabs. When she's done she curls around me and goes to sleep. She doesn't untie me. She doesn't give me my turn to cum. But she's left my penis inside of her so I wiggle my hips beneath her until a small pathetic orgasm drips out.

I sigh and try to get comfortable. The Christmas lights on the tree at the foot of our bed and the antlers poking into my chest and neck make it difficult to fall asleep.

CHAPTER THREE
COFFEE BIRDS

I awake to the sound of hooves on the ceiling.

Damn it, Christmas Eve sex always gives me nightmares. Last year I had nightmares about being a piece of candy in some kid's stocking and now I'm having dreams about reindeer on my roof.

My eyes widen. My head clears. The hooves continue scraping at my rooftop. It's not a dream anymore. I listen carefully. There are bells and animal grunts and clomping hooves.

The Christmas tree at the foot of the bed shakes. I look at it. It shakes again. I hear noises coming from the hole in the floor, belches and squishy squeaks. The tree rustles at me.

"Wake up," I whisper to Decapitron.

She snores on top of me.

I wiggle under her body and say, "Hey, come on."

She groans as she wakes.

"What's going on?" she says.

"Listen," I say.

The tree rustles and an ornament pops off of a branch and lands on our bed. She sees it and sits up.

"It's Santa," she says.

"What's he doing here?" I ask.

"What do you mean?" she says. "He comes every year..."

"Which Santa?" I ask. "Yours or mine."

"There's only one Santa," she says.

"Untie me," I say. "I wanna see."

"No," she says, pressing her cheek against my chest. "Stay here. You'll only upset him if you go down there."

"But what if it's a burglar?" I say.

"I'll annihilate any burglar that ever steps foot in this house."

Then she goes back to sleep.

I hear Angelica screaming at the top of her lungs downstairs.

Decapitron jerks awake and nearly gouges out one of my eyes with an antler.

"What's going on?" she says.

"Angelica is downstairs," I say.

"Christ," she says. "Santa's going to be pissed."

She unties me and races down to intercept our kindergartener from the intruder.

I see him standing in front of our Christmas tree, oysters in hand. He's looking at the bottom of the empty stein.

"Arrrgh!" says a thick growling voice. "Who the hell drank me beer?"

It's him. It's really him. It's my wife's version of Santa. He's standing there, jiggling. He wears gray and white rather than red and white, but other than that, his clothes looks just the same as the Santa image I grew up with. His face on the other hand is quite different. It is a balloon of sausage. He has a big white beard but his nose is a gherkin and his eyes are green olives. His mouth is a gaping hole that uses walnuts for teeth.

Angelica is just staring up at him, no longer screaming. He pats her head with his Vienna sausage fingers and smiles his rotten meat hole at her.

"Here," I tell the blobby Santa, "I'll fill up your beer."

He gargles at me as I take him away from my daughter to show him where the beer tap is on the bar.

"Arr, arr, arrrgh," he says, pouring himself a glass of stout. "Thank ye very much, me laddo. I'm rarely offered drinks on Ole X-mas Eve and usually have to resort to raiding the liquor cabinets."

For some reason Santa sounds more like a pirate than I

thought he would.

"Arr, arr, arrrgh!"

He even says arrgh instead of ho.

"Drink as much as you like," Decapitron says, stepping toward the deformed creature in her sexy latex outfit.

"Aye, me lass," he says, nodding his head at her thighs. "Aye."

She vulture-smiles and bows her antlers at him.

Angelica begins to cry.

Santa approaches her and lifts her up onto his lap.

"There, there me wee lassie," he says to her. "I'm not so bad, am I? I'm just a big hot dog. How can ye be scared of a big hot dog?"

She pouts her lips at him.

"Are ye scared of hot dogs?" he asks.

"Look," he says, lifting his wiener-like index finger and shaking it in her face. In a cute baby-talk voice, he says, "Are ye scared of the hot dog? Are ye scared, munchie munchie?"

Angelica giggles at him.

"Arrgh," he says, "yer a good lassie."

He puts her on her feet and pats her butt. "Now, go on you back to bed. Have pleasant dreams and I'll leave something special for ye under the tree."

The little chainsaw angel sticks her finger in her mouth and runs up the stairs to bed.

"Aye, a sweet kid that one is," Santa says. "Ye don't mind if I take a wee break here for a while do ya?"

He leans back in a chair and lights up a corncob pipe with peppermint tobacco.

"Make yourself at home," my wife tells him.

"Good old Decapitron," he says, checking out her cleavage. "Always treats her Santa like family."

I have no idea what the fuck just happened to my reality. If I'm not dreaming, there is a strange piratey Santa made out of sausage sitting on my living room couch flirting with my wife.

I'm not exactly sure what I should do right now so I take off the antler helmet and straighten my hairdo in a mirror.

"Arrgh, the sly guy!" Santa yells at me, raising his beer stein in approval. "Your sly guy hairstyle is legendary at the North Pole."

The words flow like hot butterscotch through my ears.

"What is that?" I ask him.

"Your sly guy style," Santa says. "It is very popular amongst the elves. They be grateful ye invented it. Too bad it didn't catch on in yer neck of the woods."

I don't know if he's yanking my chain or not, but he's given me the greatest Christmas present he possibly could have given. All I ever wanted was for my hairdo to be appreciated by others. I always wanted it to catch on and become a hip new trend.

"Cheers, me lad," Santa says.

Then he chugs down his beer.

After he finishes his pipe and another beer, Santa says, "Thanks for ye hospitality, Decapitron, but I must be on me way."

He kisses her on the knuckles with his walnut teeth. Then he comes to me. "And thank you, Sly Guy Matthew Fry." He shakes my hand with Vienna sausage fingers.

"Take care, the both of ye."

He pulls out a jar of orange marmalade and digs his hand in to pull out a glob. A whistling-whoosh sound fills the air and causes Santa to drop his dollop of jam on the floor.

His tiny earholes on the sides of his face widen to the sound and his eyes roll in circles.

"No..." he says. "It couldn't be..."

Santa gloop-jiggles over to the window and peeks through the blinds.

Several whistling-whoosh sounds are coming from outside.

"Holy Christ on a cross," Santa says. "They've found me!"

Whistling-whooshes grow louder.

"Ye've got to take the children and get to safety," he says to my wife. "Go through the back door and run. Run and don't ye look back."

Decapitron runs upstairs.

I look out of the window, wondering what the heck the fuss is about. Small black blurs are flying through the air towards the house.

"What are they?" I ask him.

"Coffee birds I call 'em," Santa says. "Bastards come after me every year but they ain't found me in over a dozen decades. Me deer are just too fast for 'em."

They do look like birds made out of coffee. They are flying blobs of hot liquid that pierce through the frosty air, leaving trails of steam. One of them slices into a snowman out front, melting a hole through its icy head. The coffee bird settles inside of the snowman's brain, causing a mist to pour out of its eyes and skull. Then the snowman comes alive.

It is the one with pineapples on its head like spiky bunny ears and phone cords dangling out of its body like tentacles. The face on the snowman starts to move. Its mouth hisses. The phone cord tentacles flap into the air as it begins to slide across the snow towards the house.

More coffee birds penetrate the snowmen outside, bringing

them to life.

"What the fuck!" I say.

"Arr, ye must get out now!" Santa says.

All of the two dozen snowmen we made today are now alive and heading towards the house. The snowmen in our neighbors' yards are also coming to life and crossing the street. The coffee birds circle above, searching for more snowmen in the area.

"Yeah," I say. "I'll catch you later."

Upstairs, Nora and Angelica are putting on slippers. Decapitron has holstered the twins to her back but didn't bother changing out of her green reindeer fetish outfit.

"The snowmen, they've..." I begin.

She snaps her fingers to hurry me up.

"They've come for Sausagey Santa..."

We go downstairs. Snowballs are being pelted at the side of the house.

"It's too late, me buckaroos," Santa says, crying at us and wiping the tears away with his beard. "They've got the place surrounded."

"Don't worry, Santa," Nora says, placing her hand on his elbow. "My mom won't let anything happen to you."

"That's nice of ye to say me la—" Santa leaps away from Nora with a yelp as he notices the bloody growth on the side of her face.

Even a sausage hideous monstrosity like Santa finds Nora disturbing.

The snowman with axes for limbs begins chopping at the front door. Santa and I look at each other with squealing faces.

"Quick," he says. "Up the chimney. We'll all take me sleigh to safety."

Santa grabs the jar of marmalade and gives it to Angelica.

"Quick," he says to her. "Lube yourself up!"

Angelica pretends she knows all about lubing herself up. But, since she doesn't, she just stands there looking at it until her sister takes it out of her hand and applies it to her own body.

After Nora is finished lubing herself up she rubs the jam onto her sister and gives the jar back to Santa.

"Why are we all orangey?" Angelica asks the sausage man.

"Arrr, didn't Decapitron ever tell ye?" Santa says. "There is magic in marmalade. Just a glob of this magic jelly and you will be able to slide into any sized hole when going down. It is also sticky enough to help you climb up sheer walls when going up."

Angelica pretends she knows all about climbing sheer walls.

Santa has Nora lead the way. The deformed girl climbs up the chimney like Spiderman with her jammy palms.

"Good," Santa says.

Then he helps Angelica with her chainsaw angel wings enter the fireplace. Once she gets inside, she scurries up the chimney like a mouse.

The front door breaks away and three snowmen enter the room. One of them with axes for limbs, one of them with a twirling fan for a face, and one with a sledgehammer for a head.

Santa jumps into the fireplace and leaps into the air, squeezing himself through the chimney. After a few feet, he doesn't move anymore.

"Arrgh, I'm stuck!" Santa cries, his little sausage legs dangling above the fire logs. "I didn't use enough marmalade!"

"Help him," Decapitron says.

I go to the fireplace and push on the meat man's butt as my wife begins decapitating the snowmen with her bare feet. As the snowmen lose their heads the coffee birds flee from the broken balls of ice and retreat through the front door. Once all of the snowmen inside the house are dead empty shells, Decapitron charges into the front yard with icy fists. The twins on her back scream with excitement.

The outside battle cries dim into silence. All I can hear is Santa's muffled voice yelling at me to get him out of there.

Instead of pushing, I try pulling. I put all of my weight into it and he pops out of the chimney into my lap. Sitting in my lap, he looks up at me and smiles. Then I realize how short and plump he is. His flesh feels more marshmallowy than it does sausagey.

"What happened?" he says to me, looking around the room at the dead snowmen.

"My wife went after them," I say.

"Oh, no," Santa says, standing up and brushing fireplace ashes from his butt. "She has no idea what they're capable of."

"You have no idea what Decapitron is capable of," I tell him.

He lubes himself up better the second time. Then he lubes me up as well.

"Come, me laddo," he says.

We climb up the chimney to the roof. The marmalade really is magic. It does most of the climbing for me. All I have to do is place a goop palm on the wall of the chimney and the slime pulls me upwards.

The first thing I see when I reach my snowy rooftop is Santa's electric sleigh. It is made out of lightning, just like Decapitron said. Sparkling volts of light shimmer at me as I stand myself up. Past the sleigh are his reindeer, grunting and sneezing at each other.

Wait... Something is amiss.

My daughters are gone.

"The bastard!" Santa says. "He took it! He took me bag!"

The plump little man hops to the edge of my roof, looking off into the distance. I see it, down the street. The snowmen are fleeing the scene with Santa's giant bag. There is movement coming from inside of the bag, as well as the screams of my little girls.

I can make out what appears to be a leader of the snowmen. A large, 4-balled snowman with a row of carrots going down the back of his head like a Mohawk, large razor sharp sickles for arms, and on his face the snowman has a Hitler mustache made of coal.

"We need to go after them," I tell Santa.

"Jump in," he tells me as he blobs towards his lightning sleigh. "Let's pick up your wife first."

I step inside of the sleigh. It feels like it is made of glass. Santa snaps his reins and the carriage takes us up off the rooftop and lands gently in the front yard on a pile of snowmen corpses.

Decapitron is standing by the mail box. She isn't moving. Upon closer inspection, we discover that she has been turned to ice. Her flesh has become glassy and transparent. She's now a masterfully carved ice sculpture of herself. The twins strapped to her back have also been changed to ice.

"Frosty's magic is strong, me boy," Santa says. "She never should have tried to take him on alone."

"Is... is she dead?"

"Nay," he says. "Not yet, anyway. If we get them back to the North Pole in time they can surely be saved."

"What about my daughters?" I ask.

"We cannot save them right now," he says. "We have to regroup, bring your wife back from the ice, and then go after Frosty when we're good and ready. I have to get me bag back from the bastard. All of Christmas depends on it."

I touch my hand to Decapitron's glassy cheek.

"What do ye say, lad?" asks Sausagey Santa. "Will ye help me save Christmas from the bastards?"

Still staring at my icy wife, I nod my head.

"As long as you help me get my daughter back," I say, forgetting for a second that I have more than one daughter.

"It's a promise," he says.

CHAPTER FOUR
SKY GRAVES

Heading towards the North Pole:

My ice sculpture of a wife is propped against the backseat of the sleigh where Santa's bag of presents should be. I try my hardest to keep my hairdo together as we fly through the air at light speed, hoping Decapitron doesn't slip out of her seat and shatter on the ground below.

"Who was that snowman, anyway?" I ask Santa.

"Arrr, that be Frosty The Neo-Nazi Snowman of Satan," he says. "Or Nazi Frosty for short. He be me arch nemesis for ages, always trying to ruin Christmas for all the kiddies. Always praising Satan instead of Baby Jesus."

Santa tells me the story of how Frosty came into being.

Frosty actually came from Santa himself. After Kris Kringle attempted suicide for the last time and became the sausagey mutant he is today, he decided he wanted to change. He wanted to figure out a way to change his opinion of Christmas so that his eternity wouldn't be such a living hell. The elves agreed to help him and together they created a machine that could expel all of the hate out of his mind. The hate was sucked out of Kringle's brain tissue through vacuum tubes. When sucked out of the brain, hate looks like steaming hot black coffee. They extracted enough hate coffee to fill five bathtubs. When it was all over, Kringle was free of his hatred and soon became the happy piratey character sitting next to me.

Unfortunately, Kringle is 100% immortal. And by 100% I mean that not any tiny piece of him can ever die. Not even his hate. Though it was separated from him, the hatred did not die.

It just lingered, stewed, until it eventually took on a life of its own. It grew its own consciousness. It became a new immortal life form. It became Frosty.

Frosty's true form is five bathtubs of steaming black hate coffee, but over time he learned how to separate his mass into coffee birds. He learned how to possess the bodies of snowmen. He learned how to control ice and bend nature to his will.

Besides being a big Hitler fan, Frosty thinks Satan is number one. His major goals include: promoting the anti-Christ, creating an anti-Christmas movement, and becoming the world's first anti-Santa. He currently resides at the South Pole where he is building an enormous concentration camp for children.

We're starting to pass through grave space. It is a popular new thing to be buried in mid-air rather than underground. Tombstones and coffins have anti-gravitation devices planted on them so they can hover in the sky. Santa navigates slowly through the floating graveyard, careful not to crash into anyone's coffin. The night is calm and gentle as we swim through. The dead drift back and forth like hundreds of baby cradles floating in the middle of the sea.

One of the sky graves comes so close to the sleigh that it nearly bonks me in the head. I get a good look at the words on the tombstone. They read: "She loved the stars too fondly to be fearful of the night." Just like the song by that old surrealistic rock band The Slow Poisoners.

She also loved the stars so fondly that her family buried her in them. It probably cost them a pretty penny as well. Sky burials are not cheap.

It doesn't take us too long to get to the North Pole, but it sure didn't seem like we were going at the speed of light. Perhaps the sleigh has the ability to travel at the speed of light but never does because the wind force would peel Santa's face off of his head and meat gravy would spill out onto the houses below.

In the distance, there are towers made of ice. They are jagged and spiky. Like a forest of glass crab legs. There is a whole city of people down there. No, not people. They are elves.

"Arr, arr, arrrrgh!" Santa says.

I still have to get used to him saying that instead of *ho, ho, ho*.

He gives me a big walnut smile as he takes us in for a landing.

Upon landing, the sleigh gets swarmed by hundreds of elves. Their voices are like millions of locust wings flapping through the air. Three of the elves approach us as we step down from the seats of lightning.

They are only four feet tall but very thin with long pointy ears. They aren't at all as plump and munchkin-like as I was expecting. All three of them wear dark green business suits with white shirts and red ties, carrying clipboards with pens flipping through their tiny fingers. One of them is a bald elf with a white handlebar mustache. Another elf is a female with a white pixie haircut. And the third elf has a white... SLY GUY HAIRCUT!

He catches my eyes and we both slick back our hair at each other. Then we snap and point finger-guns at one another. This guy is sly. I like him.

"What is the problem?" Pixie Elf asks Santa. "You've barely completed the second quadrant."

"He smells of beer," Bald Elf says. "Are you flying drunk again?"

Their voices are all mousey and squeaky.

"Nay, nay!" Santa says. "Well... aye. Aye, I had a few to drink.

But that's not why I be comin' round. We've a major emergency tonight. Frosty the Nazi bastard done stolen me bag of toys."

The elf crowd's locust-flapping voices rise so loudly they sound like an avalanche.

"Me pal, de one and only Sly Guy Matthew Fry, is here to help." As Santa speaks, the elves clamor with amazement at his words, whispering *It's the Sly Guy!* or some say *Oh, wow, Matt Fry!* "Frosty has kidnapped his children and we have to fight to get them back."

I had no idea I was famous anywhere, let alone the North Pole. I look out among the crowd of elves and see dozens of sly guy haircuts. They aren't quite as slick as my 'do, but are still pretty sweet.

The elves carefully take Decapitron out of the backseat and put her on a greasy black octopus-shaped cart. The tentacles of the octopus squirm towards the ground as if it's alive.

"They'll be fine, lad," Santa says, as the cart squirt-drives her away to one of the glass buildings in the distance.

I notice there aren't a lot of colors around here. I was expecting the North Pole to be filled with bright lights and colorful buildings. It seems like the place would be more like a giant toy box. But everything is white and black and gray. The elves even have white hair and light gray skin. The only color is in the clothing worn by the elves.

Bald Elf climbs a spiral staircase that leads to an icicled steel platform.

"Elves," Bald Elf says to the crowd. "Frosty has committed an act of war. He has stolen Santa's bag in an attempt to foil Christmas. We will not stand for this."

Bald Elf breaks a tiny icicle off of his handlebar mustache. He holds it with his index finger and his thumb and points it up at the sky like a tiny sword.

"Elves," he continues. "Tonight we go to war!"

The elves cheer. They begin a chant: "Fight for Christmas! Fight for Christmas! Fight for Christmas! Fight for Christmas!"

Bald Elf stabs his icicle up and down with every syllable of the chant.

Sausagey Santa nods his balloon of a head at the crowd of elves and winks at me with his green olive eyes.

CHAPTER FIVE
HYPERSPACE PANTIES

We board a small rust-colored train and take it deep inside of the crystal facility. Bald Elf stays behind to organize the elven troops. Sly Guy Elf sits next to me, bobbing his head in a cool groove. Most of the elves don't wear green suits like Pixie Elf and Sly Guy Elf. They wear red shirts under green overalls, sometimes wearing white aprons. Pixie Elf and Sly Guy Elf must be the managers.

"It's so dreary here," I tell Santa in the seat across from me. "I was expecting it to be a happier, more colorful place."

"The arctic be a harsh environment," Santa says. "It is not a very happy place."

The color does not improve as the train enters the facility. The lighting is dim. The walls are gray and white. Every once in a while we will pass something Christmassy, like a giant plastic candy cane or a frosted wreath, but they are so few and far between that the bright colors just give a feeling of loneliness.

Many of the elves are looking back at me, to check out the original sly guy hairstyle. Some of the guy elves point finger-guns at me and I wink back at them. Many of the girl elves look at me, swoon, and giggle. I wink at them, too.

"They like ye," Santa whispers to me. "There's plenty of time before we leave if ye want to take 'em to bed."

"Huh?" I ask.

"Elves be total sluts," Santa says. "They never shy away from a good pump in the arse. Go on, give 'em a try."

"Huh? No!" I say. "Decapitron would annihilate me."

"Aye, but technically she's dead at the moment," he says. "For the time being, ye be a swingin' single bachelor again. How's she ever going to know?"

"No, thanks," I tell him. "There's no way I'll ever cheat on my wife with an elf."

"Arrr, ye breakin' me heart, laddie," Santa says. "And ye breakin' de elves' hearts, too. They don't have much to do up here for fun in the North Pole but have sex, ye know? They would've loved to have rammed crotches with the inventor of the sly guy haircut himself."

The train stops in a muddy red movie theater. All of the seats are empty, but a Burt Reynolds movie is playing on the screen.

"Let's get it together, people," Pixie Elf squeaky-says to the crowd of elves exiting the train. "We need weapons, we need armor, we need magic spells."

Magic spells?

"Meet back here in ninety minutes," she says.

"Fight for Christmas!" the elves cry.

"Go with Tea and Boon," Santa tells me, motioning to Pixie Elf and Sly Guy Elf. "They'll help ye with preparations."

"What about you?" I ask.

"I got me own preparations to deal with."

He blobs up the aisle of the movie theater and exits to the right.

All the elves spread out in different directions. A few of the sly guys point gun-fingers at me when they pass. I wink at them and groove up the steps behind Tea and Boon.

"This way," Boon says.

He snaps his finger and spins on his heels to change directions.

"That was pretty sly," Tea says to Sly Guy Elf.

And Boon knows he's sly. He bobs his head as he walks.

The facility is much like the insides of an office building, but it is very cold, dim, and drab. The floor is concrete and the walls have framed pieces of notebook paper with pencil scribbles on them. It seems like such a dull and lonely place.

"What do you elves do for fun around here?" I ask.

"There's not a lot to do," says Tea. "We mostly have to use our imaginations."

"Imaginations?"

"Yeah," she says. "We tend to role play a lot. You know, like Dungeons and Dragons."

"Elves are awesome at Dungeons and Dragons," Sly Guy Elf says.

"I've got this 40th level wizard with a cloak of magic winds," Tea says.

"My fighter/thief can walk through walls!" Boon says.

"I've got a ring of necromancy!"

"I've got some gauntlets of ogre strength!"

They are beginning to get really excited about all this D&D talk. On the walls, I realize that the framed pieces of notebook paper are actually character sheets. Engraved into the frames are the words "Warrior of the Week" with a name and date.

All of the characters are of the elf race. There aren't any dwarves or gnomes or halflings or humans. I wonder if Santa's elves wish they were more like the Dungeons and Dragons elves. Maybe they wish they were taller and more agile. Skillful with the bow and quick with a sword. Masters at conjuring mystical spells.

"Come on," Tea says, pulling me by the arm. "I'll show you the costume I wear to the Sword and Serpent Ball!"

Damn it. What the hell just happened?

One second I was on my way to get ready for battle so that I can save my children from the forces of darkness and the next second I'm sitting in an elven dormitory waiting for a couple of elves to come out of the bathrooms so they can show me what they look like when dressed up as their Dungeons and Dragons characters.

What a complete waste of time. I don't even like Dungeons and Dragons. Sure, I used to play it in college. Who didn't? But it's just not my thing anymore. Adventuring is cool. I understand that. But these days I like real life adventure. You know, like what Spelunker sings about. Who cares about dragons and paladins when that stuff doesn't even exist? Fighting anacondas in the jungle while militia snipers are coming after you and there's ancient Aztec treasure in your satchel and a hot Latin babe that needs saving... now that's something I can role play.

Tea comes out first wearing her mage's costume.

The little elf pretends that I'm not in the room as she poses with her staff and crystal ball. It's not all that impressive of a costume. She's basically just wearing a silver bikini, a white cloak, high silver boots that go past her knees, and a large necklace with dangling plastic shards that are probably supposed to be magic crystals.

She slowly swings her staff around her head, trying to be sly. I'm not sure if she's waiting for a reaction from me or what, but she keeps moving as gracefully as she can across the floor in front of me. I adjust myself in the tiny elf chair, trying to get comfortable. I might be here for a while.

Tea eventually looks at me. Probably annoyed with my lack of excitement for her costume. She steps slowly towards me like she thinks she's a sexy runway model. Once she gets up close to me, she seductively places her boot on the arm of my chair.

"Pretty hot, huh?" she squeaky-says.

I almost shrug at her but decide to nod instead.

She puts down her leg and then leans her hip at my face.

"Look," she says, pointing at a tag on her bikini bottom. "They're hyperspace panties."

"What are hyperspace panties?" I ask.

"I'll show you," she says.

I'm beginning to get scared.

Very scared.

The little elf woman is staring at me in her wizard costume. She has one of her gray elf hands inside of her panties and appears to be masturbating. Her other hand on my knee.

I have no idea what's going on. She's supposed to be showing me what hyperspace panties are but she's just masturbating, blowing her white bangs out of her face so she can stare at me with her wide black eyes. What the hell is wrong with elves anyway? And the worst part is I think I'm getting an erection.

Elf eyes are pretty weird. I don't know what else to do, so I look into her eyes and try to hide the fact that I'm getting a hard-on. Her eyes are black. There isn't that much of the white part showing because the black circles are so wide. The freaky thing is that there's a white swirl that starts at the center of the pupil and spirals out. Like they are meant to hypnotize people. Her eyes don't hypnotize me, though. They just freak the hell out of me.

"Ready?" she says.

I raise my eyebrows at her.

Then she pushes a tiny button on the side of her panties and both of us jump. I scream as something squeezes around my penis. Tea screams too, joyfully. Her eyes look up at the ceiling and her mouth curls into a smile.

"What the hell?" I say.

Something moist is inside of my pants, tightening around my penis.

Tea looks at me. She starts humping the air in my direction. As she moves, the moist pressure inside of my pants moves with her.

"Understand?" she says, giggling.

She's fucking me. I don't know how, but it's like her hyperspace panties have the ability to cut through space and warp my penis directly into her vagina without the rest of our bodies touching.

"Stop it," I tell her.

She just smiles and humps the air.

I get out of the chair and run across the room.

"Cut it out!" I scream.

Then she really starts to get into it, closing her eyes tight and fucking me from across the room. I unzip my pants and shriek. My penis is missing. There is a blue light with white static in the place where my penis used to be. I can feel it, but can't see it. The skin around the blue is pumping up and down.

"You can't get away," she says, grabbing her crotch, "no matter how far you run. Once you've been homed in, you're stuck inside until I release you."

"Let me go!" I say.

She just laughs at me with her squeaky voice and continues humping the air.

Great. First, I'm forced to check out some Dungeons and Dragons costumes and now I'm being raped by an elf. Decapitron isn't going to understand this at all.

I go to the far side of the room and bump into Boon. He's wearing chainmail armor and a horned helmet that's probably ruining his sly guy haircut.

"What do you think?" he says.

Over his shoulder, I see Tea thrashing in the air on the other side of the room. She begins screaming at the top of her lungs, squeezing her vaginal muscles tight around me as she orgasms. It causes me to close my eyes and lean against a wall as I start cumming inside of her.

Tea stops screaming. She drops into a chair and leans her head back, wheezing.

I pause for a moment to look at the floor, panting.

Then I look back at Boon and say, "Great. It's just great."

He bobs his helmeted head at me as if he knows that I was just having hyperspace-sex and thinks I played it off pretty slyly.

We go to Tea. She's draped over the chair with a big smile from elf ear to elf ear. Her head turns and she pierces into me with her big swirly eyes. It's crazy to think that I just had a very intimate moment with this creature from across the room. I haven't even seen what she looks like naked.

"It's time to get ready for battle," Boon says.

"To battle!" Tea says, raising her tiny fist into the air.

CHAPTER SIX
CABBAGE SKIN

Tea has her arm wrapped around me as we walk down the hallway to the armory. She nods at all of the elf girls we pass. They look at us and giggle. I think Tea is showing me off like I'm a trophy. Like she's saying, "Not only did I just have sex with a human, I had sex with *the* Sly Guy!" And all of the other elves are jealous.

Decapitron is going to annihilate me.

I jerk my arm away from Tea's hands, but she just grabs it again and hugs it close to her chest. There's another group of elves down the hall that she wants to show me off to. Looking down at her, I notice that her gray skin has a slight lavender glow to it. She didn't have that before. None of the other elves have it. That's probably how all the elves know that we've just had sex. I bet whenever elves have an orgasm their skin changes color. Or maybe they change color so that they can attract a mate like certain bugs and animals do. I don't really care to know.

The armory isn't really an armory. It seems more like a supply closet containing a bunch of Dungeons and Dragons costumes.

"What kind of weapon do you want?" Boon asks. "A battleaxe? A warhammer? A broad sword of telepathy +1?"

"I don't want to get so close," I tell them. "Give me something I can shoot."

"Like a crossbow?" Tea asks.

"No, none of that Dungeons and Dragons stuff," I say.

Their faces droop into sadness.

"Something more hi-tech," I say. "At least a gun."

"Regular bullets won't be very useful," Tea says. "What you need is a flamethrower."

"We can give him the cabbage suit," Boon says.

"Yeah," Tea says. "The cabbage suit will fit good."

"Cabbage suit?"

"It's the perfect weapon," the pixie elf says. "Though... hmmm... it's not designed for humans."

"The shrinkulator!" Boon says.

"Yeah," Tea says. "The shrinkulator will make it fit."

Tea and Boon pick out swords, spears, and shields for themselves and then take me upstairs to another section of the facility. This area is wide open and mostly empty except for large white machines sticking out of the walls. Boon snaps his finger and tries to spin on his heel to change directions, but with the bulky armor he doesn't come off as very sly. He goes through a door on the right to get the cabbage suit. Tea takes me over to a group of tables and picks up a big black device that looks kind of like a glue gun.

"Okay, hold still," Tea says.

She points the gun at me and turns it on. I jerk as a white beam shoots out of the gun into my chest. Looking down, the beam isn't causing any damage. It just makes my skin feel all tingly.

I look up at the elf and see that she is growing. No, wait, I am shrinking. She sprays me with the beam of light until I am the same size as her, then she turns it off.

"Wait..." she says.

She turns it back on and shrinks me another three inches, so that I'll be shorter than she is. Then she smirks at me.

"Very funny," I say.

"Now you're elf-size," she says. "The cabbage suit should fit perfectly."

"Why didn't you just grow the cabbage suit to fit my size?"
I ask.

"Because we have a *shrink*ulator," she says, holding up the
device. "We don't have a *grow*ulator. There's no such thing."

"Then how are you supposed to grow me back to my
normal size?" I ask.

"Hmmm..." She looks up at the ceiling and scratches her
chin. "I guess you can't."

"What do you mean I can't? I'm stuck this way forever?"

"Yeah, but I'm stuck this size forever, too."

"But you're an elf..."

"Look," she says. "You have more important things to worry
about right now, like rescuing your children from a satanic Nazi
snowman. Besides, you're probably going to get killed anyway."

Boon returns with the cabbage suit. It looks like a wetsuit made
from elephant skin. It's gray and very wrinkled.

As he hands it to me, an alarm sounds.

"Time to go," he says.

"Already?" Tea asks.

The elves shake the uniform at me until I take it and put
it on over my clothes. I tighten the hood around my face and
Boon gives me a thumbs up.

"Come on," he says. "Let's go."

They race to the exit, leaving me standing here.

"So how does this thing work?" I yell.

They are too far ahead to answer.

I walk alone back to the train, getting lost in all the identical
corridors. Eventually I run into some elves and follow them to
the movie theater where another Burt Reynolds movie plays on

the screen. Elves must love Burt Reynolds.

As I board the train, random elves push me out of their way to get through. None of them realize it's the sly man in this cabbage suit. None of them are treating me like the hairdo hero anymore.

I hate being small.

On the train ride outside, I look for Tea and Boon but they aren't in my car. They never told me how to work the cabbage suit.

What the hell does it do, anyway? It's just a big wrinkly baggy suit.

I ask the white-bearded elf sitting next to me, "How does it work?"

But he just frowns at me like I'm some kind of elven retard.

When I exit the train, the elf army has gathered in the frozen moonlight.

My wife, Bald Elf, and Sausagey Santa are standing in the center of the crowd next to Santa's sleigh. Santa is wearing a giant rocket pack and has swords and laser cannons strapped to him. Decapitron is still wearing her reindeer fetish outfit but she has large candy canes holstered to her back where the twins used to be.

I push my way through the elven crowd towards them.

"Decapitron!" I cry.

When I arrive, she has no idea who I am.

"It's me," I say, taking off the cabbagey hood.

"Fry?" she says. "What the hell happened to you?"

"The stupid elves shrunk me," I say. "So I can fit into this suit."

"What the hell kind of suit is that?" she asks.

"It's a cabbage suit," I say.

"What's it do?" she asks.

"I have no idea," I say.

She frowns at my new size and taps me in the chest with her toe, pushing me back. Now she hardly needs to use any strength at all to knock me around.

"Where's the twins?" I ask.

She turns around to show me them sleeping in the back of Santa's sleigh.

I turn around to see Tea and Boon standing next to me. Tea's skin is still glowing lavender. She stands a little too close to me. I want to ask her how the suit works, but I don't want my wife to know that I've been hanging around with her just in case she knows why elven skin changes color.

Tea smacks my butt when Decapitron isn't looking.

I am so going to get annihilated.

CHAPTER SEVEN
DISEASE TRAIN

Decapitron, the twins, Santa, myself, and five elves ride in the sleigh. They make me sit in Santa's lap to make room for some of the elves. A lavender elf with a white Burt Reynolds mustache sits in Decapitron's lap. When I see him my head jerks a double-take and then I notice how cozy and friendly the two of them look together.

"Why are you all purple?" I ask Burt Reynolds Elf.

He and Decapitron just laugh at me like it's an in-joke. Then she vulture-smiles at him.

I'm glad I cheated on her while she was dead.

The rest of the elven army take their own transports, which are all made out of lightning like Santa's sleigh. But they are all different shapes and sizes. Some of them are shaped like sea serpents coiling through the air. Others are like squids. Others are starfish-shaped. Some, like the seahorse-shaped transports, carry only a single elf. Others, like the turtle-shaped transport, can carry dozens of elves. All of their lightning transports seem to be shaped like sea creatures.

"Fight for Christmas! Fight for Christmas!" the elves on the other transports chant.

The manager elves, like Boon and Tea, are on their own ships. They have to lead the troops into battle. I wish they were here to explain my cabbage suit. I don't care if Decapitron sees me talking to Tea anymore.

I look up at Santa.

"Do you know how this suit works?" I ask Santa.

"What that be?" he asks.

"A cabbage suit," I say.

"Never heard of it," he says.

Besides Burt Reynolds Elf, there are four other elves in the sleigh. Three of them are males and one female. Of the males: one has a pig nose, one has a big white unibrow, and one has his sleeve rolled up so he can show off a tough skull tattoo on his arm. As for the female, she has very long white hair and Asian eyes.

Santa's lap is strangely comfortable. His sausage thighs are squishy and form-fitting around my butt. However, there is an odd havarti smell rising out of him that makes my nostrils shudder.

A storm cloud comes towards us as we pass over New York City. The twins are looking over the edge at the bright lights of the city. Their cotton candy hair blows in the wind.

"Arrr, this might get a bit bumpity," Santa says as we approach the storm.

The cloud opens up and dumps piles of snow onto the streets below.

"Hmmm..." Santa says, squinting his eye-olives at the storm.

The cloud poofs up into a big round pillow of white and then a face forms inside. Black eyes, a black mouth, and a fluffy nose with a Hitler mustache dangling off the end.

"It's a trap!" Santa screams, as the cloud face opens up its mouth and blows a gust of wind at our fleet of ships.

The sleigh dives down under the gust, but several transports get hit. A lightning sea turtle tips over and dozens of elves tumble through the wintry night. The fleet scatters. Lightning stingrays and seahorses slice through the air around us as we dive down between the buildings.

The giant head of Frosty comes after us. It lowers down into the city and squeezes through the New York high-rises, spitting hundreds of snowballs at us like a Tommy Gun. A lightning shark crashes into a building on our right and explodes. A lightning squid plummets toward the street from above, tentacles flailing as it falls.

"Ye bastard!" Santa cries at the giant fluffy blob.

The lightning sea creatures crash and explode all around us. The snowy New York streets are littered with their flaming husks, as well as the mutilated bodies of a hundred elves dressed in Dungeons and Dragons outfits.

We have only one advantage: the cloud moves very slowly.

"Full speed!" Santa yells to Bald Elf who drives the big electric serpent-shaped transport.

Bald Elf nods as seahorse ships spin sideways through the air around him. He pushes forward on his joystick controls, which I guess are what steer his ship. As the snaking vehicle speeds up, a tumbling lightning crab beheads the serpent and Bald Elf is vaporized in the explosion. The passengers on the lightning snake shriek as it coils down to earth.

Santa whacks the reins and his deer speed up, pulling us far away from the Hitlery storm cloud.

I look back. Only half a dozen ships are left behind us. Tea's squid ship is still afloat, but I don't see Boon.

In the distance, Frosty's giant head-shaped cloud curls its mouth downwards. Then a long smoke hand extends out of the top of his head and forms the devil sign, as he evaporates over the city.

"It's a good thing those elves are immortal," I tell Santa.

"Nay, me boy," Santa says. "Elves be as mortal as you. They live long, but they die as good as any being. Only I and Frosty be the eternals in this war."

Our broken fleet makes it to Antarctica without another incident. Unibrow Elf tells Santa that Boon's ship, as well as several other ships, are still in the air. Most of them were scattered in different directions and got off course. Boon says he will rally them back together and meet us at the South Pole.

Over Antarctica, we pass a collection of crystal train tracks that hover in midair.

"What are those?" I ask Santa.

"Those are for the disease train," Santa says.

The disease train carries dead bodies from America into Antarctica. Frosty uses his power over winter winds to pull the bodies of those buried in sky graves down into the Antarctic. The bodies are then put on disease trains and brought to the South Pole.

Once the corpses are frozen in the Antarctic climate, they can be possessed by coffee birds. Then they can join the ranks of the F.N.S.A. (Frosty's Nazi Satany Army).

The train is up ahead, chugging on its tracks. It's so high off the ground it looks like it's flying.

"There it be," Santa says.

He squishes one of his Vienna sausage fingers into a button on the dashboard. Loud bursts echo against the side of the sleigh and then two lollypop rockets shoot out from underneath us. They fly across the crystal tracks and then explode upon impact.

The disease train catches on fire and drops from the sky,

disappearing into the white powder below.

"There it go," Santa says.

I'm freezing by the time we arrive at the South Pole. The cabbage suit doesn't provide any extra warmth and Santa's heater is breaking down.

The frozen city of the South Pole is much bigger than the elven city of the North Pole, but it is even more drab and dark. Instead of elves, this city is populated by hundreds of F.N.S.A. zombies and wicked snowmen. We get in a little closer before all the zombies start to howl. They scream with their rotten frozen lungs as if some kind of signal.

"Tentacle bombs," Santa tells me. "Push it. Quickly, lad."

But I don't understand what he's talking about.

Santa groans and pushes the button himself. Bombs drop out of the bottom of the sleigh. As the bombs hit the ground they burst open and large black tentacles explode out of the containers. The tentacles swell and stretch, wrapping around the zombies and crushing their throats. Their howls subside.

"We don't want them warning the others," Santa says.

"I thought they all had one consciousness," I say. "If one of them saw us wouldn't all of them see us?"

"Nay, me laddo," he says. "Once they split they become separate entities. They don't share their minds until the coffee is brought back together into one pool. If we tread carefully we might still be able to catch them by surprise."

75

CHAPTER EIGHT
THE GRINDING STATION

"There it be," Santa says. "Frosty's domain. The grinding station."

Ahead I see a large black structure. It is a mess of grinding machinery. Gears and spikes and blades and cylinders chew at the air like metal jaws. Steam pours out of horns on its head.

"My kids are in there?" I ask.

"Aye," he says. "But we'll get them. Ye shall see, me boy."

A massive icicle shoots out of the black metal structure like a harpoon and impales a starfish ship on our left. The icicle is attached to a chain that quickly retracts, ripping the ship back into the grinding station. The elves shriek as they are eaten alive by the machine's crushing jaws.

"Attack!" Santa screams.

He launches five wreath-shaped missiles that spin through the air like Frisbees and explode in the mouth of the grinding station. No visible damage.

Several icicle harpoons are launched at us. Santa jerks at the reindeer and they dodge out of the way. The harpoons catch two more elf ships and reel them in. The elves jump from their seats and fall to their deaths to avoid being eaten by the grinding station.

Santa fires toy train-shaped missiles at it. No effect. More icicles are launched. Dozens this time.

"Retreat!" Santa cries.

A harpooned clam-shaped ship smashes into us, ripping through the side of the sleigh and slamming into the reindeer, as it gets reeled in by the grinding station.

The sleigh is going down.

We spiral out of control as the clam ship is crunched into the machine. Santa and the elves wail into my ears, even Decapitron cries out, as we descend.

The sleigh slams hard into the snow at the foot of the grinding station. The elves are grunting and groaning in the backseat. I look up to see the last couple of elven ships fleeing from the harpoons and escaping the frozen city.

Santa straightens himself and widens his ear holes at the air. I hear it, too. There is a leaking sound. Like someone is going to the bathroom. Then I see it. One of the reindeer. Its belly has been torn open and it is leaking fluid. By the smell of it, I'd say the fluid is gasoline.

The olive-eyes on Santa's face grow so wide the pimentos almost pop out.

"Run!" he cries.

We jump out and run in opposite directions away from the sleigh. Once I'm at a safe distance, I turn around. The reindeer just stands there casually for a few minutes, huffing and stomping its hooves, as it leaks gasoline from its guts.

Then the reindeer explodes.

It causes a chain reaction and each of the reindeer explode one at a time.

Santa stands above me with tears pouring down his cheeks. As the reindeers detonate into balls of flame, he names them off one by one, crying, "Now, Dasher. Now, Dancer. Now, Prancer and Vixen. On, Comet. On, Cupid. On Donner and Blitzen," until the explosions reach the sleigh.

When the sleigh explodes, lightning spiders into the snowscape all around us. It crawls up the grinding station and electrocutes the steel structure until its gears lock up and its jaws droop open with chained harpoons drooling out down its chin.

We might have lost the sleigh and the reindeer but at least we've paralyzed the grinding station.

We regroup around the flaming sleigh. Burnt deer flesh fills the air.

"How are we going to get home?" I ask Santa.

"Me poor darlings," he says, his eyes lost in the fire.

"We must push on," Unibrow Elf says.

"Let's focus on recovering the bag first," Asian Elf says. "Then we'll worry about getting home."

The other elves nod at her in agreement.

"Frosty's going to pay for all this," says Burt Reynolds Elf, as the living dead fill the streets.

The zombies come at us from all sides, emptying out of the icy buildings nearby.

"There's too many of them," squeals Pig Nose Elf. "We should run."

"No way," Burt Reynolds Elf says. "We're going to fight!"

Burt Reynolds Elf pulls two sawed-off shotguns from holsters on his thighs. Unlike the other elves, he doesn't much care for the Dungeons and Dragons thing. He wears boots and a navy blue shirt tucked into his jeans.

The zombies dive towards him as he steps out into the open, but Burt Reynolds Elf dodges out of the way and blows their heads off at point blank range. He kills them two at a time. Their skulls become splatters of red mulch sprayed across the fresh snow. When the shotguns need to be pumped, he slams the butts of the guns against zombie foreheads while holding the pump, cocking it in the process. Then he shoots two more.

I hate to admit it, but:

Burt Reynolds Elf = fucking awesome.

Decapitron joins him. She takes a candy cane from her back and pulls on the crook of the cane. A blade slides out like a cane sword. A candy cane sword?

She charges into the zombie crowd head-first and skewers one of them with her antlers. Then she decapitates another with her candy cane sword. The twins are strapped to her back, giggling as she slices off heads and severs limbs.

The other elves don't seem to be as tough as Burt Reynolds Elf. They stay behind, like me. They have swords and axes in their hands, but they don't have any idea what they're supposed to do with them. Well, except for the one with the skull tattoo. He is fidgeting with some kind of gadget in a backpack. Maybe it's a bomb or something.

"What do we do?" I ask them.

They look at me like I'm supposed to have the answers.

"Fight for Christmas?" Pig Nose Elf asks.

I shrug at him.

"You do something," Unibrow Elf says. "You've got the cabbage suit."

"Do you know how to use it?" I ask.

"No," he says.

He looks at the other elves, but they all just shrug at him.

Skull Tattoo Elf gets his gadget working and buckles his backpack on. It makes a loud whirring noise like that of a lawnmower. His gadget is some kind of vacuum cleaner. A hose leads from its mouth into his backpack.

"Rock!" he tells me.

I wonder if Skull Tattoo Elf listens to adventure rock...

He points his vacuum on the horde of zombies and they back away from him. His weapon sucks the black coffee out of the corpses' eyes. He goes after several of them at a time. Once all of the black coffee is pulled out of a zombie its body goes limp and falls to the ground.

"This guy knows what he's doing," I tell the other elves.

They nod and we stay close behind him for safety.

The bodies pile up in the snow as Skull Tattoo Elf sucks the life out of the undead creatures. I can't see Decapitron or Burt Reynolds Elf, but I can hear gunshots and the whooshing of swords on the other side of the burning sleigh. Zombies swipe at Santa as he continues to cry for his fallen reindeer, but he doesn't seem to care.

Coffee birds that have exited the bodies of Decapitron's victims fly over the sleigh towards us. Skull Tattoo Elf tries to vacuum them up in midair, but many of them get through. They dive into the hollow bodies lying in the snow and we find ourselves surrounded by more zombies.

Asian Elf shrieks as a rotten claw rips into her stomach. Teeth tear into her neck and rip open her arteries, spraying black blood into the wind. Elves have black blood?

Skull Tattoo Elf points his mouth at her attacker and sucks the coffee bird out of its eyes, but he's too late. She's already dead.

"Into the grinding station," Skull Tattoo Elf says.

We fall back, dodging the zombies to get into the black metal building. The corpses tower over me. I'm hobbit-sized now and won't have the strength to break free if any of them clutch onto me. Unibrow Elf and I clear the horde, but Pig

Nose Elf becomes entangled in a forest of rotten arms.

"Help!" he cries. "Not me!"

Skull Tattoo Elf turns back, but there are too many of them. Pig Nose Elf disappears into the sea of massive corpses. His screams become choking coughs as black blood fills his lungs.

"Santa, come on!" I yell.

Santa is just standing there as corpses attack him. They rip open his sausage casings. Meat goo empties out into the snow.

"It's no use, me lad," he cries. "The sleigh is destroyed. The children won't get their presents this year."

"Come on!" I say.

Skull Tattoo Elf pulls me away as he sucks coffee birds out of eye sockets.

We circle the metal structure until we find the entrance. It's electronically locked, but Unibrow Elf cracks the thirty-eight digit code so fast that it looks like he has twenty hands at work on the lock.

When the door opens, he winks at me and gives me a finger-gun with a click of his thumb.

That was pretty sly of him.

Once inside, we shut the door behind us to keep the zombies out. The others are still out there but they didn't follow us. I don't know what Decapitron's problem is. We're here to save our kids, not kill a bunch of zombies to impress an elf with a Burt Reynolds mustache. I feel like we've really been growing apart ever since she died.

There is a spiral staircase leading up to the brain of the facility.

"Come on," Skull Tattoo Elf says, leading the way up the steps.

Upstairs, we arrive in a large dark room. There is crying coming from the shadows.

"What's that?" Unibrow Elf asks.

We follow the crying to a big box in the center of the room. There are barred windows on the sides of the box. The crying comes from within. I recognize that sound.

"Angelica?" I ask, peeking through the window.

I see her in there, curled around her big sister.

She looks up at me and jumps to her feet.

"Hi, Sly Fry!" she cries.

"My angel!" I say. "Don't worry, the Sly Guy's here to rescue you!"

Nora doesn't say anything. She's weak. It looks like her wound has drooled a lot of blood. A puddle fills the floor of the box.

I look at Unibrow Elf. "How do we open it?" I ask him.

Unibrow Elf examines the cage, looking it up and down.

"The top," he says.

We can't reach the top of the cage. The window is near the bottom, but the top stretches twelve feet into the air.

"I'll get it," Skull Tattoo Elf says.

He grips the vacuum tube with his mouth and climbs the side of the box. Once he gets up there, he examines the top. Doesn't see anything. He crawls across the lid and then looks at me and shrugs.

"Angelica, how did you get in?" I ask. "The top?"

She shakes her head.

"Where then?" I ask.

She points at the window in the back.

Unibrow Elf and I circle their prison to the back window.

"Ahh," Unibrow Elf says, nodding at the barred window here.

He pulls a latch and the window unlocks. But as it unlocks the room fills with a clanking sound.

"What's that?" Unibrow Elf says.

We listen carefully. It is coming from the cage. It sounds almost like... music.

I look up. A crank on the side of the box is turning, almost like a...

"Get off of there!" I yell at Skull Tattoo Elf.

He looks down at me. "Huh?"

The music stops and the lid of the box bursts open, sending Skull Tattoo Elf into the air. He crashes into the ceiling and his neck snaps. Then his limp body falls to the ground with a plop.

I look up as a giant head turns to face me. It bobs up and down on its coiled neck.

The jack-in-the-box doesn't have the usual clown head, nor the pointy hat and pointy nose. Its head is a grotesque collection of body parts, frozen together into the shape of a head. I can see coffee birds swimming within its pinhole eyes.

Unibrow Elf and I run away from it as the head hisses and slurps at us with the dismembered torso it uses for a tongue.

It swings its head and the box jumps off the ground towards us. My daughters scream inside, as it begins hopping across the room. Unibrow Elf turns around to see how far away it is. The jack-in-the-box locks eyes with him and then speeds up, hopping three times hyper fast and then up high. Unibrow Elf cowers on the ground as the box smashes down on him, flattening him into a black sticky paste that oozes out from beneath the cage.

The girls scream high-pitched as the jack hops after me. I stop and turn back. It locks eyes with mine and then charges at me. It hops three times fast and then goes up high over my head, covering my vision in shadow. But I roll out of the way behind its back before it gets me.

I run for Skull Tattoo Elf's body and remove his backpack. The meaty jack doesn't realize that it didn't crush me. It bobs in the corner of the room, basking in its supposed victory. Once I get the backpack on, I flip the vacuum's switch and it whirs up.

The Frankenstein head jerks at me and hisses. I see inside of its mouth and realize that there are a dozen hands at the back of its throat. Since the jack doesn't have any vocal chords, the hands rub their palms together really fast to create the hissing noise.

The jack charges at me, but I circle it with my vacuum pointed up. Black liquid drains out of its eye sockets towards me. Coffee birds attempt to flee from the jack, but the vacuum has them in its pull. The jack attempts one more jump at me, but I cartwheel out of the way. When the sockets are sucked dry, the chunky head drops against the side of the box, its torso-tongue dangling out of its leg-lips.

The girls cheer and clap for me.

I do a moonwalk dance for them with gun-fingers pointing in the air. Then I do another cartwheel. It's easy to do acrobatics when you're small.

I help Nora and Angelica out of their cage.

"Why are you so short?" Angelica asks.

"Elf magic," I say.

"You're smaller than me," Nora says.

"I've always been smaller than you," I say.

CHAPTER NINE
CLOCK SAUSAGE

I take my daughters downstairs and exit the grinding station.

Outside, there is a giant battle going on between an army of snowmen and an army of Dungeons and Dragons elves. Boon made it. He regrouped the scattered elf ships and brought them here safely.

The shredded remains of zombies are sprinkled through the snow. Decapitron must have annihilated all of them. I scan the battlefield, but I don't see antlers on any of the warriors. I can't spot Boon, Santa, or Burt Reynolds Elf either.

I hold out the vacuum to suck up any coffee birds that might be lingering in the zombie parts, just in case. I'm not taking any risks when my kids are involved.

"Well?" Nora says.

"What?" I ask.

"Well, go fight," she says.

"I'm guarding you," I say.

"Cowards guard," she says. "Heroes fight."

"You didn't think I was a coward when I saved you back there," I say.

She rolls her eyes at me like I don't know what I'm talking about. The growth on her head pulses with the movement of her eyes.

I see Tea near the corner of the grinding station. She's stabbing at a snowman with a spear, but it doesn't seem to be doing any good.

"Come on," I tell my kids.

I sneak up behind Tea and vacuum the coffee bird out of her opponent.

She turns around.

"You!" she says.

"Hi," I say.

"Why aren't you using your cabbage suit?" she asks.

"Nobody told me how it works," I say.

"You should be fighting Frosty with Santa," she says.

I shrug at her.

"I was rescuing my kids," I say.

"Here," she says, pointing at my vacuum weapon. "Give me that. I'll look after your kids for you."

She tells me how to use the cabbage suit and then points me in the direction of Santa and Frosty. Before I go, Angelica gives me a kiss on the cheek.

"I can reach you now!" she says, happy with my new height.

I snap a gun-finger at her and groove my way into the battlefield backwards.

Backwards!

I mean, how sly is that?

Dodging through snowmen armed with icicle swords and ice cube shields, I make it into a large intersection of the city where Santa and Frosty are battling out their final showdown.

Burt Reynolds Elf is nearby. He's kneeling against a building, holding his wounds. Black blood drips over his fingers.

"Where's my wife?" I ask him.

He points behind me.

Decapitron is staggering towards us, dragging her candy

cane sword through the snow. Her latex outfit is all sliced up with deep gashes in her chest and shoulders. One of her antlers is missing. As she arrives, she leans all of her weight on my shoulder and nearly crushes me. She's almost twice my size now. I can't hold her up anymore.

"How're the twins?" I ask.

I go behind her. The boys are gurgling at each other. They look down at me and smile. I smile back and wink at them. I go to give Matty a cootchy-cootchy-coo on the bottom of his foot, but there's nothing there. His foot has been cut off.

"What the hell?" I cry.

"What?" Decapitron moans.

"His foot's gone!" I cry.

"So," she says, annoyed with me. "He'll live."

"He's just a baby! You got his foot cut off!"

She shrugs. "It's fine."

"What kind of mom are you?" I say. "You fight zombies with your babies on your back!"

"What kind of dad are you?" she says. "You're four feet tall."

Burt Reynolds Elf laughs. He doesn't seem to notice he's about the same height as me.

"I'm the kind of four feet tall dad who just saved his daughters," I say.

She makes a farting noise with her lips at me. It's almost as if she's drunk. She only acts this way towards me when she's drunk. Then I notice a large wound on her head where the antler used to be. She's probably got a concussion. She isn't thinking straight.

I turn back to look at the battle.

It looks like Sausagey Santa must have gotten his nerves back after the reinforcements arrived. He is sliced up, dripping meat paste in the snow as he fights. His hat and white hair are missing, leaving just a balloon of sausage for a head. In one hand he fights with a large saber and in the other he has one of those vacuum weapons. He cuts at Frosty and sucks at his black soul liquid as well.

But Frosty is in good shape. Whenever Santa cuts off any of his snow flesh, he just replenishes it with the snow from the ground. Whenever Santa vacuums some coffee out of his eyes, there are always more coffee birds in the air to join the pool inside his head. But when Santa gets hit by Frosty's large sickle arms, the sausage that is lost cannot be refilled.

Santa's going to need my help for this battle. I pull my arms inside of my cabbage suit and find the controls, hoping I remember what Tea told me to do.

"Hmm..." I say to myself, trying to find the right buttons without being able to see them.

A scream fills the air as Frosty cuts Santa in half.

Sausage legs wiggle on the ground as Santa's torso crawls away from the snow man. He still sucks at him with his vacuum, but he's lost his sword.

I better help him now.

"Hitler was a wussy vegetarian!" I scream at Frosty.

There was nothing else I could think of to say to get Frosty's attention, but it works.

I step away from Decapitron and groove into the middle of the street, the empty sleeves of my suit dangling at my sides. Frosty just snarls at me as I center myself.

Okay, here it goes...

I push one of the buttons and the suit curls my body up

into a ball. The cabbage skin ignites around me and then I launch myself at Frosty.

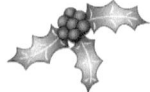

I can hardly imagine what I must look like out there. I am a big fireball rolling through the snow at 70 miles per hour, melting everything in my path. On the control switch between my legs, there's a little monitor. I see Frosty's mouth open wide with shock as I plow into him, dissolving his bottom ball. Rolling around and coming back towards him, I see him trying to reform the snowball with the snow from the ground but I hit him again. He explodes into powder.

Meanwhile, the upper half of Santa is vacuuming up Frosty's coffee birds. But he doesn't get all of them as Frosty's consciousness leaves his body and enters a nearby snowman. The new snowman retrieves the sickle-arms and the Hitler mustache and becomes his old self, good as new.

But there's no stopping the sly man. I melt his new body just as quickly as the last one, rolling in circles around the intersection. Santa sucks up more of his coffee birds.

I roll and I roll until all the snowmen in the area have turned to liquid and all of the coffee birds have been sucked away.

By the time I finish rolling in circles and figure out how to make the suit get out of fireball form (Tea didn't explain that part to me), I find myself in the middle of a crowd of elves. They explode with cheers for me. They hoot and applaud and cheer.

"Hooray for the sly guy!" they sing. "He's the greatest! Sly Fry's number one!"

Santa gets restuffed with old clocks. It's not sausage, but it'll have to do for now until the elves find the rest of his meat goop that's been splattered all over the South Pole. He recovers his bag of toys and then the elves build him a new sleigh out of Tea's squid ship.

"Arrr, ye know what?" Santa says. "I might just be able to save Christmas this year."

The elves cheer for him.

"Sorry, laddie," Santa tells me. "No time fer thanks and pleasantries. I need to deliver toys to the rest of the boys and girls of the world."

"Can we come with you?" I ask.

"Can we, Santa?" my kids cry. "Can we?"

Santa looks down at Nora's bloody growth dripping into the snow.

"Nay..." he says. "The elves will give ye a ride home."

"But Santa..." Angelica cries.

"Please?" I say.

"Well..." Santa says. "You know what?... it's really late and I really don't have time for this kind of bullshite right now. I know ye saved me from the forces of evil and all, but come on, man. I've been cut in half and most of me guts have been replaced with clocks for Christ's sake. I've never had a worse Christmas in all me life."

Before I can say another word his squidy vehicle blasts off, leaving me in a cloud of snow.

Boon leads us towards another ship so he can give us a ride home.

"Don't worry," he tells me. "I'm sure he'll leave you something special under your tree tomorrow."

CHAPTER TEN
PRESENT WORMS

Christmas Morning:

I wake up at home, alone in my bed.

I'm not sure how I got here. I don't remember the trip back from the South Pole.

It was all so much like a dream. I would think none of it really happened if it wasn't for the distance between my feet and the edge of the bed. Being elf-sized, our queen bed feels bigger than a king.

It's already the afternoon. Not really Christmas morning anymore, it's Christmas Day. I get up and put on a robe. Then wander into the bathroom.

Boon is standing on a stool, grooving to a tune in his head while shaving in the mirror.

"You're awake," he says.

I groan.

"You've missed out on all the presents," he says.

I shrug at him and urinate into the toilet. My brain feels sore inside my head.

After I'm done I just stare at him for a while, watching him shave.

Then I say, "What are you doing here?"

He waits until he's finished shaving to answer me.

"You know how I said Santa was probably going to leave you special presents under the tree for Christmas?" he says, hopping off of the stool.

"Yeah," I say.

"Well, he's decided to give each member of your family the

gift of your dreams," he says. "And he's here to give them to you personally."

Boon leads me out of my room and takes me downstairs.

As I look over the balcony, I see all the surviving elves lounging around on my furniture. Above them, Angelica is flying around the living room with chainsaw angel wings. The chainsaws buzz as her wings flap.

"Angelica?" I say.

She opens her mouth in excitement when she sees me and flies in close. "Look at me, Sly Guy! I'm a real angel! Look at me!"

"See," Boon says. "She got the gift of her dreams. She can now fly like an angel."

I wish I would have explained to Angelica that angels don't really use chainsaws for wings.

I go down the stairs and pass the twins. They are running around the dining room table. Well, one of them is running. Matty is hopping on one foot.

"What did they get?" I ask.

"They were given the gift of free movement. They were sick of being strapped to your wife all the time. They wanted to be able to run and play, but couldn't. So that's what Santa gave them."

"Did Nora get her brain chip?" I ask. "Or, no, if she could have anything I bet she'd want her growth removed..."

"No," he says. "That's not what she wanted."

"What did she want, then?"

"She wanted to become the dictator of a small third-world country."

"Sounds like Nora," I say.

"So, what did I get?" I ask. "I see I didn't get my old height back. That's all I really want. Please exchange whatever Santa gave me with my old height."

"We'll see," he says.

Tea barges between us, wearing one of my old shirts as a dress and drinking out of my favorite coffee mug.

"Santa has your present out back," she says.

Then she continues on her way. As she passes, she purposely rubs her breasts against me. They feel nice. I check out her body as she walks away. For some reason, I find her pretty sexy now that I'm at this shrunken down height. She doesn't creep me out like she did at the North Pole. I don't feel so bad about being raped by her anymore.

My path outside is blocked by a giant robot.

A big transformer toy is standing eighteen feet off the ground in my backyard, leaning against the side of the house. I guess my wife wanted a real transformer for Christmas...

Boon and I squeeze through the transformer's legs. It is a big female transformer with torpedo boobs.

"Sly Fry," Boon says. "Let me introduce you to your new wife. *The* Decapitron."

"Decapitron?" I ask.

"Hi, Fry," she says. Her voice is electronic, but it is still her voice. Her mouth doesn't move, but a light flashes on and off when she talks. "Check me out."

She transforms. The noise she makes while transforming is the same as the noise from the cartoon show. Then she is a big nuclear submarine in the backyard.

"Pretty nice, huh?" the submarine says. It isn't all that big of a submarine, but fills a good portion of our yard. The hatch on top of the submarine opens up and Burt Reynolds Elf climbs out.

He waves at me. Just great. Not only am I permanently elf-sized, but now I'm married to a giant robot. Sure Decapitron always had the personality of a giant evil robot, but now she looks like one too.

"Ready for your present?" submarine Decapitron says.

Burt Reynolds Elf helps Sausagey Santa out of the miniature nuclear submarine and they climb down to greet me. Santa is still worn and tattered, with clock-filled thighs.

"Merry Christmas, me boy," Santa says, handing me a very light present about the size of a shoe box. "Ye shall love it, I'm right sure."

I doubt I'll love it.

I rip off the wrapping paper, which is strangely covered in pictures of plump German sausages with big red bows tied around them. It is a shoe box. I open the box to find that it is empty except a small yellow piece of paper on the bottom of the box.

The paper has two words on it: turn around.

So I turn around.

HOLY MOTHER OF FUCKING CHRIST.

Oh, my fucking shit...

Can it really be?

Can it?

Is it real?

NO WAY!!!

In my backyard... MY backyard. They're here...

SPELUNKER!!!

The band Spelunker is on a stage in my yard. All five members. They are even wearing their awesome adventure gear. One of them is wearing mountain climbing gear, one is wearing snow gear, one is wearing scuba gear, one is wearing desert camo, and the singer is wearing jungle survival gear with a machete.

They pick up their guitars and wail on them.

"This is for the sly guy, Matthew Fry," says the singer, Maxwell Stone.

I point guns at him and bob my head.

HUGE smile on my face.

Then they play "Canyon Kayaking Danger Team," my absolute favorite song!

All of the elves come out of the house and dance to the rockingest tune ever written. I groove in the center of the crowd and show off my sly moves, hoping Maxwell Stone catches a glimpse of them. Angelica flies in the air above, waving down at me. I point her some gun-fingers. Even Decapitron dances in the background in her enormous robot form.

After a few songs, I go to Santa.

"How did you know?" I ask. "How did you know this is what I wanted?"

"Arrr, me boy," he says. "That be Santa's little secret."

I give him a high-five on his hotdog fingers and go back to dancing.

Between songs, Boon tells me Santa didn't actually know I wanted Spelunker to play at my house for Christmas. He says that Santa never knows what anyone wants for Christmas. Only the present worms do.

Present worms are small gooey elf-manufactured creatures that Santa uses to get boys and girls what they want for Christmas. All he does is put the worms inside of a box, address the package, and put it under the tree. While the children sleep, the present worms read their minds and find out what gift is wanted. Then the worms construct that gift, die, and evaporate before morning.

Santa's job is to figure out the size of the box and how many present worms he should put in. He decides this by calculating how naughty or nice the child has been. If he puts in only a couple of worms the present won't be very good. If he puts in six to ten it is likely to be an awesome Christmas for the little kid.

But for the members of my family Santa put three shovelfuls of present worms into each of our boxes. It was hundreds of times more potent than any present he has ever given before. There were so many worms that they could have given us any gift we ever could have wanted in the world.

I don't know about the rest of the family, but I sure got what I wanted.

The party rages on into the night. Spelunker keeps playing nonstop and the elves keep dancing. We finish all the booze in the house and Santa wraps up a bunch of present worms to make himself some scotch. He's looking for some bigger boxes so they can make a few kegs. They tell me that we're going to party nonstop for days. That's what they do every Christmas Day, after their job for the year has been completed. They like to celebrate. But this year they have to party extra hard because they have to celebrate the lives of those elves fallen in battle and celebrate the defeat of Nazi Frosty.

I'm hopping up and down like a kid, chugging some brandy eggnog. Being this size has some advantages. I sure get drunk really easily.

"This was the best Christmas ever!" Decapitron says, robot-dancing far above me.

"Yes, it was," I tell her. "The best Christmas ever!"

But I'm really drunk and probably don't mean it.

EPILOGUE

You know what they say about what house guests and dead bodies have in common, right?

Yeah, they both start to smell bad after a few days.

The party lasts a few weeks. After it's over, nobody goes home. Sausagey Santa lounges around the house in his underwear, eating eggs without taking them out of the shells. The elves keep following me around, bobbing their heads and slicking back their sly guy haircuts. They kind of view me as their sly guy leader. It was cool for awhile, but it has gotten pretty annoying as of late. Even Spelunker is starting to annoy me. They are still rocking in the backyard nonstop all day and night. I'm really starting to get sick of their music. They play the same songs over and over again. They don't eat or sleep. I've been trying to give them food and water, but they're rocking so hard they don't notice. The rhythm guitar player has passed out from exhaustion. I think he might be dead.

Angelica accidentally cut off Voltron's left hand with her chainsaw wing, so now both twins have that three-limbed thing going on. At least they've evened out.

I don't see much of Decapitron. She spends all of her time with Burt Reynolds Elf, which is fine with me. They have sex while she's in submarine form, somehow. The submarine hatch is the transformer's equivalent of a vagina I think. Every time I see him he is glowing purple. And I think he has recently gotten his nipples pierced.

Tea is pregnant with my half-elf baby. Hyperspace panties rape sex is a surefire way to get an elf pregnant. It could have been worse, though. I could have gotten some kind of weird elf STD. We've started sleeping together. My real wife can't fit inside of the house, so Tea has decided to take her place. She talks way too much about Dungeons and Dragons, but at the moment she's the only person in this house that I care to talk to.

I've been staying as far away from my family as possible. Their Christmas miracles might be a pleasure to them, but they scare the hell out of me. Christmas is supposed to bring families closer together, but this year it seems to have torn us apart. I'm not sure what's going to happen to us. I have a feeling that Santa is going to just force the whole family to move to the North Pole to live with him. Not because he wants us there but because transformers and chainsaw angels don't have a place in the civilized world. Decapitron probably won't officially divorce me, but I think she's planning on marrying Burt Reynolds Elf. Tea is assuming that we will also get married now that we have a baby coming.

It'll be odd to live the rest of my life up at the North Pole, but it probably won't be any worse than how things used to be. Life changes and goes on. It might not get any better, but it goes on. Your kids grow up. You grow old. Your children bury you. Then they grow old. Repeat. Repeat. Repeat. That's just the way it is. For everyone.

Everyone, that is, except for Santa there, sitting on the sofa with his corncob pipe and eggy breath, dripping sausage grease from rips on his skin like tears from a dead womb.

BONUS SECTION

This is the part of the book where we would have published an afterword by the author but he insisted on drawing a comic strip instead for reasons we don't quite understand.

I hope you like my book, *Sausagey Santa.* Wasn't it Christmasy?

It's me CM3!

Christmas was always my favorite holiday as a kid.

I think it's probably because it's the most common time of year to see dancing tacos in the streets.

I also like how the moon drinks Hello Kitty themed cocktails.

And Santa makes all homeless people smell like two scoops of bubblegum ice cream for a whole week.

Yay! The homeless smell yummy again!

The only part I don't like is when Jesus comes down and kills everyone on his chainsaw motorcycle.

THE
END

ABOUT THE AUTHOR

Carlton Mellick III is one of the leading authors of the bizarro fiction subgenre. Since 2001, his books have drawn an international cult following, despite the fact that they have been shunned by most libraries and chain bookstores.

He won the Wonderland Book Award for his novel, *Warrior Wolf Women of the Wasteland*, in 2009. His short fiction has appeared in *Vice Magazine, The Year's Best Fantasy and Horror #16, The Magazine of Bizarro Fiction*, and *Zombies: Encounters with the Hungry Dead*, among others. He is also a graduate of Clarion West, where he studied under the likes of Chuck Palahniuk, Connie Willis, and Cory Doctorow.

He lives in Portland, OR, the bizarro fiction mecca.

Visit him online at **www.carltonmellick.com**

Bizarro Books

CATALOG   SPRING 2013

**ERASERHEAD
PRESS**

Swallowdown

Press

Your major resource for the bizarro fiction genre:

WWW.BIZARROCENTRAL.COM

Introduce yourselves to the bizarro fiction genre and all of its authors with the Bizarro Starter Kit series. Each volume features short novels and short stories by ten of the leading bizarro authors, designed to give you a perfect sampling of the genre for only $10.

BB-0X1
"The Bizarro Starter Kit" (Orange)
Featuring D. Harlan Wilson, Carlton Mellick III, Jeremy Robert Johnson, Kevin L Donihe, Gina Ranalli, Andre Duza, Vincent W. Sakowski, Steve Beard, John Edward Lawson, and Bruce Taylor. **236 pages $10**

BB-0X2
"The Bizarro Starter Kit" (Blue)
Featuring Ray Fracalossy, Jeremy C. Shipp, Jordan Krall, Mykle Hansen, Andersen Prunty, Eckhard Gerdes, Bradley Sands, Steve Aylett, Christian TeBordo, and Tony Rauch. **244 pages $10**

BB-0X2
"The Bizarro Starter Kit" (Purple)
Featuring Russell Edson, Athena Villaverde, David Agranoff, Matthew Revert, Andrew Goldfarb, Jeff Burk, Garrett Cook, Kris Saknussemm, Cody Goodfellow, and Cameron Pierce **264 pages $10**

BB-001 **"The Kafka Effekt" D. Harlan Wilson** — A collection of forty-four irreal short stories loosely written in the vein of Franz Kafka, with more than a pinch of William S. Burroughs sprinkled on top. **211 pages $14**

BB-002 **"Satan Burger" Carlton Mellick III** — The cult novel that put Carlton Mellick III on the map ... Six punks get jobs at a fast food restaurant owned by the devil in a city violently overpopulated by surreal alien cultures. **236 pages $14**

BB-003 **"Some Things Are Better Left Unplugged" Vincent Sakwoski** — Join The Man and his Nemesis, the obese tabby, for a nightmare roller coaster ride into this postmodern fantasy. **152 pages $10**

BB-005 **"Razor Wire Pubic Hair" Carlton Mellick III** — A genderless humandildo is purchased by a razor dominatrix and brought into her nightmarish world of bizarre sex and mutilation. **176 pages $11**

BB-007 **"The Baby Jesus Butt Plug" Carlton Mellick III** — Using clones of the Baby Jesus for anal sex will be the hip sex fetish of the future. **92 pages $10**

BB-010 **"The Menstruating Mall" Carlton Mellick III** — "The Breakfast Club meets Chopping Mall as directed by David Lynch." - Brian Keene **212 pages $12**

BB-011 **"Angel Dust Apocalypse" Jeremy Robert Johnson** — Meth-heads, man-made monsters, and murderous Neo-Nazis. "Seriously amazing short stories..." - Chuck Palahniuk, author of Fight Club **184 pages $11**

BB-015 **"Foop!" Chris Genoa** — Strange happenings are going on at Dactyl, Inc, the world's first and only time travel tourism company.
"A surreal pie in the face!" - Christopher Moore **300 pages $14**

BB-032 **"Extinction Journals" Jeremy Robert Johnson** — An uncanny voyage across a newly nuclear America where one man must confront the problems associated with loneliness, insane dieties, radiation, love, and an ever-evolving cockroach suit with a mind of its own. **104 pages $10**

BB-037 **"The Haunted Vagina" Carlton Mellick III** — It's difficult to love a woman whose vagina is a gateway to the world of the dead. **132 pages $10**

BB-043 **"War Slut" Carlton Mellick III** — Part "1984," part "Waiting for Godot," and part action horror video game adaptation of John Carpenter's "The Thing." **116 pages $10**

BB-047 **"Sausagey Santa" Carlton Mellick III** — A bizarro Christmas tale featuring Santa as a piratey mutant with a body made of sausages. 124 pages $10

BB-048 **"Misadventures in a Thumbnail Universe" Vincent Sakowski** — Dive deep into the surreal and satirical realms of neo-classical Blender Fiction, filled with television shoes and flesh-filled skies. **120 pages $10**

BB-053 **"Ballad of a Slow Poisoner" Andrew Goldfarb** — Millford Mutterwurst sat down on a Tuesday to take his afternoon tea, and made the unpleasant discovery that his elbows were becoming flatter. **128 pages $10**

BB-055 **"Help! A Bear is Eating Me" Mykle Hansen** — The bizarro, heartwarming, magical tale of poor planning, hubris and severe blood loss...
150 pages $11

BB-056 **"Piecemeal June" Jordan Krall** — A man falls in love with a living sex doll, but with love comes danger when her creator comes after her with crab-squid assassins. **90 pages $9**

BB-058 **"The Overwhelming Urge" Andersen Prunty** — A collection of
bizarro tales by Andersen Prunty. **150 pages $11**

BB-059 **"Adolf in Wonderland" Carlton Mellick III** — A dreamlike adventure that takes a young descendant of Adolf Hitler's design and sends him down the
rabbit hole into a world of imperfection and disorder. **180 pages $11**

BB-061 **"Ultra Fuckers" Carlton Mellick III** — Absurdist suburban horror
about a couple who enter an upper middle class gated community but can't find their way
out. **108 pages $9**

BB-062 **"House of Houses" Kevin L. Donihe** — An odd man wants to marry
his house. Unfortunately, all of the houses in the world collapse at the same time in the
Great House Holocaust. Now he must travel to House Heaven to find his departed fiancee.
172 pages $11

BB-064 **"Squid Pulp Blues" Jordan Krall** — In these three bizarro-noir novellas, the reader is thrown into a world of murderers, drugs made from squid parts, deformed gun-toting veterans, and a mischievous apocalyptic donkey. **204 pages $12**

BB-065 **"Jack and Mr. Grin" Andersen Prunty** — "When Mr. Grin calls
you can hear a smile in his voice. Not a warm and friendly smile, but the kind that seizes
your spine in fear. You don't need to pay your phone bill to hear it. That smile is in every
line of Prunty's prose." - Tom Bradley. **208 pages $12**

BB-066 **"Cybernetrix" Carlton Mellick III** — What would you do if your
normal everyday world was slowly mutating into the video game world from Tron? **212
pages $12**

BB-072 **"Zerostrata" Andersen Prunty** — Hansel Nothing lives in a tree
house, suffers from memory loss, has a very eccentric family, and falls in love with a
woman who runs naked through the woods every night. **144 pages $11**

BB-073 **"The Egg Man" Carlton Mellick III** — It is a world where humans reproduce like insects. Children are the property of corporations, and having an enormous ten-foot brain implanted into your skull is a grotesque sexual fetish. Mellick's industrial urban dystopia is one of his darkest and grittiest to date. **184 pages $11**

BB-074 **"Shark Hunting in Paradise Garden" Cameron Pierce** — A group of strange humanoid religious fanatics travel back in time to the Garden of Eden to discover it is invested with hundreds of giant flying maneating sharks. **150 pages $10**

BB-075 **"Apeshit" Carlton Mellick III** - Friday the 13th meets Visitor Q. Six hipster teens go to a cabin in the woods inhabited by a deformed killer. An incredibly fucked-up parody of B-horror movies with a bizarro slant. **192 pages $12**

BB-076 **"Fuckers of Everything on the Crazy Shitting Planet of the Vomit At smosphere" Mykle Hansen** - Three bizarro satires. Monster Cocks, Journey to the Center of Agnes Cuddlebottom, and Crazy Shitting Planet. **228 pages $12**

BB-077 **"The Kissing Bug" Daniel Scott Buck** — In the tradition of Roald Dahl, Tim Burton, and Edward Gorey, comes this bizarro anti-war children's story about a bohemian conenose kissing bug who falls in love with a human woman. **116 pages $10**

BB-078 **"MachoPoni" Lotus Rose** — It's My Little Pony... *Bizarro* style! A long time ago Poniworld was split in two. On one side of the Jagged Line is the Pastel Kingdom, a magical land of music, parties, and positivity. On the other side of the Jagged Line is Dark Kingdom inhabited by an army of undead ponies. **148 pages $11**

BB-079 **"The Faggiest Vampire" Carlton Mellick III** — A Roald Dahl-esque children's story about two faggy vampires who partake in a mustache competition to find out which one is truly the faggiest. **104 pages $10**

BB-080 **"Sky Tongues" Gina Ranalli** — The autobiography of Sky Tongues, the biracial hermaphrodite actress with tongues for fingers. Follow her strange life story as she rises from freak to fame. **204 pages $12**

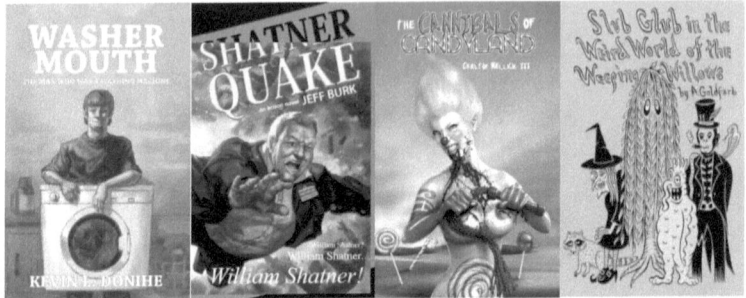

BB-081 **"Washer Mouth" Kevin L. Donihe** - A washing machine becomes human and pursues his dream of meeting his favorite soap opera star. **244 pages $11**

BB-082 **"Shatnerquake" Jeff Burk** - All of the characters ever played by William Shatner are suddenly sucked into our world. Their mission: hunt down and destroy the real William Shatner. **100 pages $10**

BB-083 **"The Cannibals of Candyland" Carlton Mellick III** - There exists a race of cannibals that are made of candy. They live in an underground world made out of candy. One man has dedicated his life to killing them all. **170 pages $11**

BB-084 **"Slub Glub in the Weird World of the Weeping Willows"** **Andrew Goldfarb** - The charming tale of a blue glob named Slub Glub who helps the weeping willows whose tears are flooding the earth. There are also hyenas, ghosts, and a voodoo priest **100 pages $10**

BB-085 **"Super Fetus" Adam Pepper** - Try to abort this fetus and he'll kick your ass! **104 pages $10**

BB-086 **"Fistful of Feet" Jordan Krall** - A bizarro tribute to spaghetti westerns, featuring Cthulhu-worshipping Indians, a woman with four feet, a crazed gunman who is obsessed with sucking on candy, Syphilis-ridden mutants, sexually transmitted tattoos, and a house devoted to the freakiest fetishes. **228 pages $12**

BB-087 **"Ass Goblins of Auschwitz" Cameron Pierce** - It's Monty Python meets Nazi exploitation in a surreal nightmare as can only be imagined by Bizarro author Cameron Pierce. **104 pages $10**

BB-088 **"Silent Weapons for Quiet Wars" Cody Goodfellow** - "This is high-end psychological surrealist horror meets bottom-feeding low-life crime in a techno-thrilling science fiction world full of Lovecraft and magic..." -John Skipp **212 pages $12**

BB-089 "Warrior Wolf Women of the Wasteland" Carlton Mellick III
— Road Warrior Werewolves versus McDonaldland Mutants...post-apocalyptic fiction has never been quite like this. **316 pages $13**

BB-091 "Super Giant Monster Time" Jeff Burk — A tribute to choose your own adventures and Godzilla movies. Will you escape the giant monsters that are rampaging the fuck out of your city and shit? Or will you join the mob of alien-controlled punk rockers causing chaos in the streets? What happens next depends on you. **188 pages $12**

BB-092 "Perfect Union" Cody Goodfellow — "Cronenberg's THE FLY on a grand scale: human/insect gene-spliced body horror, where the human hive politics are as shocking as the gore." -John Skipp. **272 pages $13**

BB-093 "Sunset with a Beard" Carlton Mellick III — 14 stories of surreal science fiction. **200 pages $12**

BB-094 "My Fake War" Andersen Prunty — The absurd tale of an unlikely soldier forced to fight a war that, quite possibly, does not exist. It's Rambo meets Waiting for Godot in this subversive satire of American values and the scope of the human imagination. **128 pages $11**

BB-095 "Lost in Cat Brain Land" Cameron Pierce — Sad stories from a surreal world. A fascist mustache, the ghost of Franz Kafka, a desert inside a dead cat. Primordial entities mourn the death of their child. The desperate serve tea to mysterious creatures. A hopeless romantic falls in love with a pterodactyl. And much more. **152 pages $11**

BB-096 "The Kobold Wizard's Dildo of Enlightenment +2" Carlton Mellick III — A Dungeons and Dragons parody about a group of people who learn they are only made up characters in an AD&D campaign and must find a way to resist their nerdy teenaged players and retarded dungeon master in order to survive. 232 **pages $12**

BB-098 "A Hundred Horrible Sorrows of Ogner Stump" Andrew Goldfarb — Goldfarb's acclaimed comic series. A magical and weird journey into the horrors of everyday life. **164 pages $11**

BB-099 **"Pickled Apocalypse of Pancake Island" Cameron Pierce**—A demented fairy tale about a pickle, a pancake, and the apocalypse. **102 pages $8**

BB-100 **"Slag Attack" Andersen Prunty**— Slag Attack features four visceral, noir stories about the living, crawling apocalypse.A slag is what survivors are calling the slug-like maggots raining from the sky, burrowing inside people, and hollowing out their flesh and their sanity. **148 pages $11**

BB-101 **"Slaughterhouse High" Robert Devereaux**—A place where schools are built with secret passageways, rebellious teens get zippers installed in their mouths and genitals, and once a year, on that special night, one couple is slaughtered and the bits of their bodies are kept as souvenirs. **304 pages $13**

BB-102 **"The Emerald Burrito of Oz" John Skipp & Marc Levinthal** —OZ IS REAL! Magic is real! The gate is really in Kansas! And America is finally allowing Earth tourists to visit this weird-ass, mysterious land. But when Gene of Los Angeles heads off for summer vacation in the Emerald City, little does he know that a war is brewing...a war that could destroy both worlds. **280 pages $13**

BB-103 **"The Vegan Revolution... with Zombies" David Agranoff** — When there's no more meat in hell, the vegans will walk the earth. **160 pages $11**

BB-104 **"The Flappy Parts" Kevin L Donihe**—Poems about bunnies, LSD, and police abuse. You know, things that matter. 132 **pages $11**

BB-105 **"Sorry I Ruined Your Orgy" Bradley Sands**—Bizarro humorist Bradley Sands returns with one of the strangest, most hilarious collections of the year. **130 pages $11**

BB-106 **"Mr. Magic Realism" Bruce Taylor**—Like Golden Age science fiction comics written by Freud, *Mr. Magic Realism* is a strange, insightful adventure that spans the furthest reaches of the galaxy, exploring the hidden caverns in the hearts and minds of men, women, aliens, and biomechanical cats. **152 pages $11**

BB-107 "Zombies and Shit" Carlton Mellick III—"Battle Royale" meets "Return of the Living Dead." Mellick's bizarro tribute to the zombie genre. **308 pages $13**

BB-108 "The Cannibal's Guide to Ethical Living" Mykle Hansen— Over a five star French meal of fine wine, organic vegetables and human flesh, a lunatic delivers a witty, chilling, disturbingly sane argument in favor of eating the rich.. **184 pages $11**

BB-109 "Starfish Girl" Athena Villaverde—In a post-apocalyptic underwater dome society, a girl with a starfish growing from her head and an assassin with sea anenome hair are on the run from a gang of mutant fish men. **160 pages $11**

BB-110 "Lick Your Neighbor" Chris Genoa—Mutant ninjas, a talking whale, kung fu masters, maniacal pilgrims, and an alcoholic clown populate Chris Genoa's surreal, darkly comical and unnerving reimagining of the first Thanksgiving. **303 pages $13**

BB-111 "Night of the Assholes" Kevin L. Donihe—A plague of assholes is infecting the countryside. Normal everyday people are transforming into jerks, snobs, dicks, and douchebags. And they all have only one purpose: to make your life a living hell.. **192 pages $11**

BB-112 "Jimmy Plush, Teddy Bear Detective" Garrett Cook—Hardboiled cases of a private detective trapped within a teddy bear body. **180 pages $11**

BB-113 "The Deadheart Shelters" Forrest Armstrong—The hip hop lovechild of William Burroughs and Dali .. **144 pages $11**

BB-114 "Eyeballs Growing All Over Me... Again" Tony Raugh— Absurd, surreal, playful, dream-like, whimsical, and a lot of fun to read. **144 pages $11**

BB-115 **"Whargoul" Dave Brockie** — From the killing grounds of Stalingrad to the death camps of the holocaust. From torture chambers in Iraq to race riots in the United States, the Whargoul was there, killing and raping. **244 pages $12**

BB-116 **"By the Time We Leave Here, We'll Be Friends" J. David Osborne** — A David Lynchian nightmare set in a Russian gulag, where its prisoners, guards, traitors, soldiers, lovers, and demons fight for survival and their own rapidly deteriorating humanity. **168 pages $11**

BB-117 **"Christmas on Crack" edited by Carlton Mellick III** — Perverted Christmas Tales for the whole family! . . . as long as every member of your family is over the age of 18. **168 pages $11**

BB-118 **"Crab Town" Carlton Mellick III** — Radiation fetishists, balloon people, mutant crabs, sail-bike road warriors, and a love affair between a woman and an H-Bomb. This is one mean asshole of a city. Welcome to Crab Town. **100 pages $8**

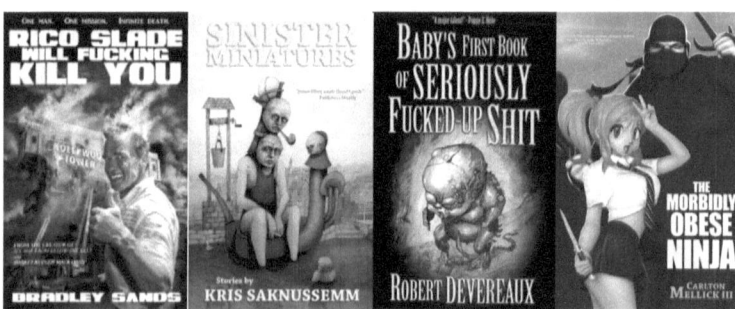

BB-119 **"Rico Slade Will Fucking Kill You" Bradley Sands** — Rico Slade is an action hero. Rico Slade can rip out a throat with his bare hands. Rico Slade's favorite food is the honey-roasted peanut. Rico Slade will fucking kill everyone. A novel. **122 pages $8**

BB-120 **"Sinister Miniatures" Kris Saknussemm** — The definitive collection of short fiction by Kris Saknussemm, confirming that he is one of the best, most daring writers of the weird to emerge in the twenty-first century. **180 pages $11**

BB-121 **"Baby's First Book of Seriously Fucked up Shit" Robert Devereaux** — Ten stories of the strange, the gross, and the just plain fucked up from one of the most original voices in horror. **176 pages $11**

BB-122 **"The Morbidly Obese Ninja" Carlton Mellick III** — These days, if you want to run a successful company . . . you're going to need a lot of ninjas. **92 pages $8**

BB-123 **"Abortion Arcade" Cameron Pierce** — An intoxicating blend of body horror and midnight movie madness, reminiscent of early David Lynch and the splatterpunks at their most sublime. **172 pages $11**

BB-124 **"Black Hole Blues" Patrick Wensink** — A hilarious double helix of country music and physics. **196 pages $11**

BB-125 **"Barbarian Beast Bitches of the Badlands" Carlton Mellick III** — Three prequels and sequels to *Warrior Wolf Women of the Wasteland.* **284 pages $13**

BB-126 **"The Traveling Dildo Salesman" Kevin L. Donihe** — A nightmare comedy about destiny, faith, and sex toys. Also featuring Donihe's most lurid and infamous short stories: *Milky Agitation, Two-Way Santa, The Helen Mower, Living Room Zombies,* and *Revenge of the Living Masturbation Rag.* **108 pages $8**

BB-127 **"Metamorphosis Blues" Bruce Taylor** — Enter a land of love beasts, intergalactic cowboys, and rock 'n roll. A land where Sears Catalogs are doorways to insanity and men keep mysterious black boxes. Welcome to the monstrous mind of Mr. Magic Realism. **136 pages $11**

BB-128 **"The Driver's Guide to Hitting Pedestrians" Andersen Prunty** — A pocket guide to the twenty-three most painful things in life, written by the most well-adjusted man in the universe. **108 pages $8**

BB-129 **"Island of the Super People" Kevin Shamel** — Four students and their anthropology professor journey to a remote island to study its indigenous population. But this is no ordinary native culture. They're super heroes and villains with flesh costumes and out-landish abilities like self-detonation, musical eyelashes, and microwave hands. **194 pages $11**

BB-130 **"Fantastic Orgy" Carlton Mellick III** — Shark Sex, mutant cats, and strange sexually transmitted diseases. Featuring the stories: *Candy-coated, Ear Cat, Fantastic Orgy, City Hobgoblins,* and *Porno in August.* **136 pages $9**

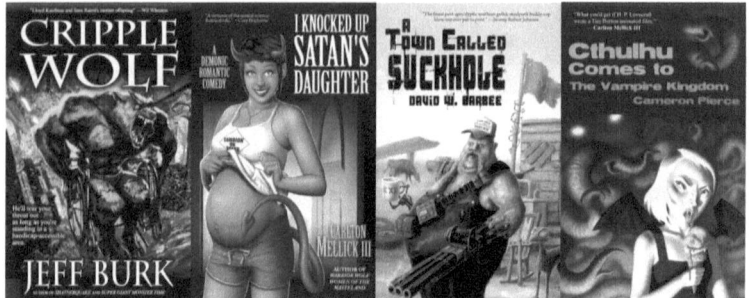

BB-131 **"Cripple Wolf" Jeff Burk** — Part man. Part wolf. 100% crippled. Also including *Punk Rock Nursing Home, Adrift with Space Badgers, Cook for Your Life, Just Another Day in the Park, Frosty and the Full Monty,* and *House of Cats.* **152 pages $10**

BB-132 **"I Knocked Up Satan's Daughter" Carlton Mellick III** — An adorable, violent, fantastical love story. A romantic comedy for the bizarro fiction reader. **152 pages $10**

BB-133 **"A Town Called Suckhole" David W. Barbee** — Far into the future, in the nuclear bowels of post-apocalyptic Dixie, there is a town. A town of derelict mobile homes, ancient junk, and mutant wildlife. A town of slack jawed rednecks who bask in the splendors of moonshine and mud boggin'. A town dedicated to the bloody and demented legacy of the Old South. A town called Suckhole. **144 pages $10**

BB-134 **"Cthulhu Comes to the Vampire Kingdom" Cameron Pierce** — What you'd get if H. P. Lovecraft wrote a Tim Burton animated film. **148 pages $11**

BB-135 **"I am Genghis Cum" Violet LeVoit** — From the savage Arctic tundra to post-partum mutations to your missing daughter's unmarked grave, join visionary madwoman Violet LeVoit in this non-stop eight-story onslaught of full-tilt Bizarro punk lit thrills. **124 pages $9**

BB-136 **"Haunt" Laura Lee Bahr** — A tripping-balls Los Angeles noir, where a mysterious dame drags you through a time-warping Bizarro hall of mirrors. **316 pages $13**

BB-137 **"Amazing Stories of the Flying Spaghetti Monster" edited by Cameron Pierce** — Like an all-spaghetti evening of Adult Swim, the Flying Spaghetti Monster will show you the many realms of His Noodly Appendage. Learn of those who worship him and the lives he touches in distant, mysterious ways. **228 pages $12**

BB-138 **"Wave of Mutilation" Douglas Lain** — A dream-pop exploration of modern architecture and the American identity, *Wave of Mutilation* is a Zen finger trap for the 21st century. **100 pages $8**

BB-139 **"Hooray for Death!" Mykle Hansen** — Famous Author Mykle Hansen draws unconventional humor from deaths tiny and large, and invites you to laugh while you can. **128 pages $10**

BB-140 **"Hypno-hog's Moonshine Monster Jamboree" Andrew Goldfarb** — Hicks, Hogs, Horror! Goldfarb is back with another strange illustrated tale of backwoods weirdness. **120 pages $9**

BB-141 **"Broken Piano For President" Patrick Wensink** — A comic masterpiece about the fast food industry, booze, and the necessity to choose happiness over work and security. **372 pages $15**

BB-142 **"Please Do Not Shoot Me in the Face" Bradley Sands** — A novel in three parts, *Please Do Not Shoot Me in the Face: A Novel*, is the story of one boy detective, the worst ninja in the world, and the great American fast food wars. It is a novel of loss, destruction, and--incredibly--genuine hope. **224 pages $12**

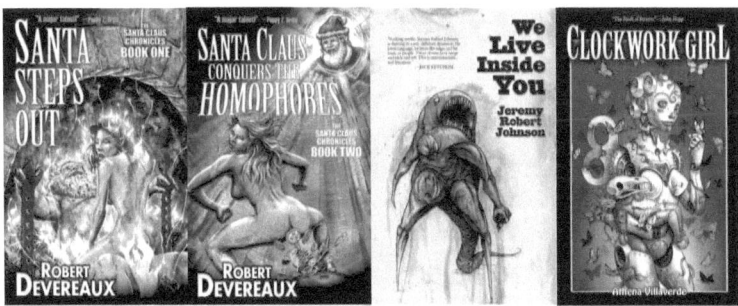

BB-143 **"Santa Steps Out" Robert Devereaux** — Sex, Death, and Santa Claus ... The ultimate erotic Christmas story is back. **294 pages $13**

BB-144 **"Santa Conquers the Homophobes" Robert Devereaux** — "I wish I could hope to ever attain one-thousandth the perversity of Robert Devereaux's toenail clippings." - Poppy Z. Brite **316 pages $13**

BB-145 **"We Live Inside You" Jeremy Robert Johnson** — "Jeremy Robert Johnson is dancing to a way different drummer. He loves language, he loves the edge, and he loves us people. These stories have range and style and wit. This is entertainment... and literature."- Jack Ketchum **188 pages $11**

BB-146 **"Clockwork Girl" Athena Villaverde** — Urban fairy tales for the weird girl in all of us. Like a combination of Francesca Lia Block, Charles de Lint, Kathe Koja, Tim Burton, and Hayao Miyazaki, her stories are cute, kinky, edgy, magical, provocative, and strange, full of poetic imagery and vicious sexuality. **160 pages $10**

BB-147 "Armadillo Fists" Carlton Mellick III — A weird-as-hell gangster story set in a world where people drive giant mechanical dinosaurs instead of cars. **168 pages $11**

BB-148 "Gargoyle Girls of Spider Island" Cameron Pierce — Four college seniors venture out into open waters for the tropical party weekend of a lifetime. Instead of a teenage sex fantasy, they find themselves in a nightmare of pirates, sharks, and sex-crazed monsters. **100 pages $8**

BB-149 "The Handsome Squirm" by Carlton Mellick III — Like Franz Kafka's *The Trial* meets an erotic body horror version of *The Blob*. **158 pages $11**

BB-150 "Tentacle Death Trip" Jordan Krall — It's *Death Race 2000* meets H. P. Lovecraft in bizarro author Jordan Krall's best and most suspenseful work to date. **224 pages $12**

BB-151 "The Obese" Nick Antosca — Like Alfred Hitchcock's *The Birds*... but with obese people. **108 pages $10**

BB-152 "All-Monster Action!" Cody Goodfellow — The world gave him a blank check and a demand: Create giant monsters to fight our wars. But Dr. Otaku was not satisfied with mere chaos and mass destruction.... **216 pages $12**

BB-153 "Ugly Heaven" Carlton Mellick III — Heaven is no longer a paradise. It was once a blissful utopia full of wonders far beyond human comprehension. But the afterlife is now in ruins. It has become an ugly, lonely wasteland populated by strange monstrous beasts, masturbating angels, and sad man-like beings wallowing in the remains of the once-great Kingdom of God. **106 pages $8**

BB-154 "Space Walrus" Kevin L. Donihe — Walter is supposed to go where no walrus has ever gone before, but all this astronaut walrus really wants is to take it easy on the intense training, escape the chimpanzee bullies, and win the love of his human trainer Dr. Stephanie. **160 pages $11**

BB-155 **"Unicorn Battle Squad" Kirsten Alene** — Mutant unicorns. A palace with a thousand human legs. The most powerful army on the planet. **192 pages $11**

BB-156 **"Kill Ball" Carlton Mellick III** — In a city where all humans live inside of plastic bubbles, exotic dancers are being murdered in the rubbery streets by a mysterious stalker known only as Kill Ball. **134 pages $10**

BB-157 **"Die You Doughnut Bastards" Cameron Pierce** — The bacon storm is rolling in. We hear the grease and sugar beat against the roof and windows. The doughnut people are attacking. We press close together, forgetting for a moment that we hate each other. **196 pages $11**

BB-158 **"Tumor Fruit" Carlton Mellick III** — Eight desperate castaways find themselves stranded on a mysterious deserted island. They are surrounded by poisonous blue plants and an ocean made of acid. Ravenous creatures lurk in the toxic jungle. The ghostly sound of crying babies can be heard on the wind. **310 pages $13**

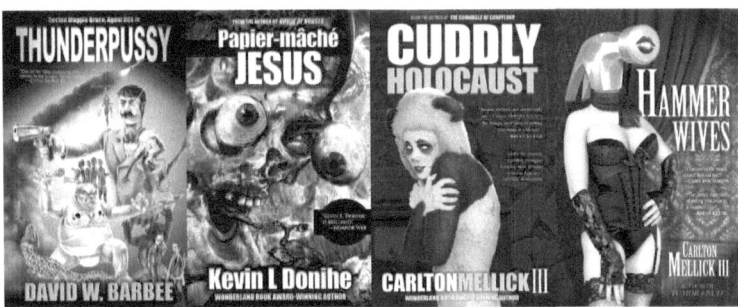

BB-159 **"Thunderpussy" David W. Barbee** — When it comes to high-tech global espionage, only one man has the balls to save humanity from the world's most powerful bastards. He's Declan Magpie Bruce, Agent 00X. **136 pages $11**

BB-160 **"Papier Mâché Jesus" Kevin L. Donihe** — Donihe's surreal wit and beautiful mind-bending imagination is on full display with stories such as All Children Go to Hell, Happiness is a Warm Gun, and Swimming in Endless Night. **154 pages $11**

BB-161 **"Cuddly Holocaust" Carlton Mellick III** — The war between humans and toys has come to an end. The toys won. **172 pages $11**

BB-162 **"Hammer Wives" Carlton Mellick III** — Fish-eyed mutants, oceans of insects, and flesh-eating women with hammers for heads. Hammer Wives collects six of his most popular novelettes and short stories. **152 pages $10**